I0677884

DESPERATE, NC

Copyright © 2025 NCSU Creative Writing MFA Program
All rights reserved

ISBN 978-1-4696-7774-3 (paperback)
ISBN 978-1-4696-7775-0 (ebook)

Cover illustration by Sam Dalzell

Published by the NCSU Creative Writing MFA Program

Distributed by the University of North Carolina Press
www.uncpress.org

Desperate, NC

The Interactive Museum Exhibition
Official Field Guide

Edited by Jendayi Brooks-Flemister, Alexander Lopez,
Cadwell Turnbull, and Misha Vaagen Lazzara

PUBLISHED BY THE NCSU CREATIVE WRITING MFA PROGRAM

Dearest Museum Guest,

Welcome! We are so pleased for you to accompany us on a journey into the heart of the fascinating world of Desperate, North Carolina. As you know, this year marks the 40 year anniversary of the public's discovery of Desperate. What follows in this exhibition will take you from Desperate's origins to the present day. What you see on this tour will undoubtedly intrigue, dazzle and delight devotees of Desperate, old and new!

Please be sure to consult this Official Field Guide, compiled by our dedicated archival museum staff, as you make your way from room to room in today's exhibition. All official museum materials are noted as such.

"Please note that merchants on and near museum premises are vending counterfeit Desperate paraphernalia. Through extensive anthropological categorizing we can assure visitors that all verifiable Desperate materials are museum property."

Note: If you purchased the upgraded holographic experience, just touch the button on the side of your glasses and a hologram of each room's unique curator will appear and introduce you to the documents exhibited. The holographic curators and this Official Field Guide will provide you with the majority of the answers to your questions. However, if you have additional questions you may direct them to any of our docents in the purple vests. You may also upgrade your original ticket to the holographic experience at any point for a small additional fee. Simply use any of the holo-glass vending machines located in the hallways between exhibits. Included in the Field Guide, you will find scans of the primary documents, and throughout the tour, you'll have exclusive access to the never-before-seen documents in their original form! These documents include letters, poems, and medical records, as well as brand new bonus content in Room #13.

Please be safe, respectful, and remember: no photography of any kind will be permitted on museum premises or at any point during your time exploring The Lost Colony of Desperate. With that said, we hope you and your loved ones have fun and learn something new and exciting today about Desperate, North Carolina.

With sincere thanks,
The Lost Colony of Desperate Exhibition Staff
August 1st, 2060

By this time, you've no doubt heard the legend of Desperate. Perhaps you've been one of the many fans who've devoured popular scholarship, or maybe you've even heard new findings disseminated by leading Desperate experts, but now, for the first time, thanks to the tireless work of our museum's archival division, you, our dear guest, will have unprecedented access to primary documents, letters, photographs, maps and interviews that have come to shape our collective understanding of The Lost Colony of Desperate and its place in contemporary history.

Many of these documents are being publicly seen and studied for the first time. As such, much of what you will see is heavily guarded behind bullet-proof glass. Please be respectful and refer to the field guide if you have trouble viewing any of the primary sources.

Desperate, NC has had a resounding influence on 21st century historians and has completely reshaped the scholarship, culture and academia of the period. More than that, the story of Desperate has captivated the hearts, imaginations and minds of millions around the world. It is our wish that what you experience today brings you not only historical first-hand accounts, entertainment, context and concrete evidence of Desperate's existence, but further brings you into the hearts and minds of the fallen members of this lost colony.

Do be warned: What follows is not for the faint of heart. For at the beginning of every tale of mystery is the violence and uncertainty at its roots.

Without further adieu, we proudly present:

THE LOST COLONY OF DESPERATE:
THE INTERACTIVE MUSEUM EXHIBITION

****Please be sure to refer to this field guide at all times, which includes the primary sources that will be referenced on your tour.*

TABLE OF CONTENTS

***NOTE FROM THE ARCHIVAL DEPARTMENT: Please be sure to follow exhibitions in designated order. You will be presented with an exhibit map at the front desk to accompany this field guide. Remember: Follow the signs above you, both in life and here at The Lost Colony of Desperate: The Interactive Exhibition. A special thanks to archival team members for providing their original research.

A Desperate Plea for Answers

Collected by Jesse Wang, Archival Team Member

Welcome to Room #1 of our tour through the Lost Colony of Desperate. What follows is an article by a member of our archival team staff, Jesse Adam Wang, whose work as a journalist in Connelly Springs remains one of the earliest accounts of Desperate before it became the global and cultural phenomenon that it is today.

The article details accounts from locals not affiliated with Desperate and shows the beginning of our conceptual understanding of the existence of Desperate.

The article discusses unnamed government sources, in which information about "magical" photos is indexed. The article details Connelly Springs locals' efforts to determine what caused the explosion.

Now, please turn your attention to the story behind the glass.

NOTES FROM NORTH CAROLINA

A DESPERATE PLEA FOR ANSWERS

After an unexplained event, local residents of Connelly Springs, NC take matters into their own hands.

BY JESSE ADAM WANG

Phillip began working at JD's Smokehouse in the spring of 2019. He told me he liked to smoke cigarettes out back where he could hear the creek running its way through the woods.

As an only child, he was used to quiet moments. And so it did not upset him when—almost a year after he'd been hired as a line cook, nearly a year of smelling like grease and barbeque every day, the scent embedded in the fabric of his clothes—he, like so many others in the food and hospitality industry, lost his job because of COVID-19.

He had some money saved. His parents had an ample garden. He told me he liked those quiet days. I visited the site where the family cabin had been built nearly a century ago. Phillip still hasn't been back there. "I can't stomach the idea of being anywhere near that place." He speaks efficiently, barely moving his lips when he talks. I didn't ask him if this had anything to do with the injuries he sustained throughout his body, including his face.

"That boy ain't said but five words to me the whole time I been knowin' him," Jonathan Divine Johnson explained to me when I visited his restaurant. JD, on the other hand, was a talker. We spent two hours together eating ribs and sipping Coors Light. I asked him about the explosion. "I was sitting right where I am now. Shit, I thought it had been an earthquake or somethin'. Hail Mary mother of Joseph I reckon I ain't been that scared before in my life!"

Phillip didn't remember much about that day. He said it was like all the other "corona days," as he called them. "Most likely I was layin' on my bed all morning. Only got up sometime in the afternoon." He told me if he had stayed in bed, hadn't decided to step out of the cabin that day, he wouldn't be alive.

On a sweltering Tuesday morning in August, nearly five hundred miles away, I visited Paul Bakery on Pennsylvania Avenue, the DOJ building framed in the coffee shop's wide glass windows. A warm croissant in front of me, I waited for my source to arrive. I will refer to them as "N."

N. had told me the LavAzza they brew at Paul is the best cup of coffee in Washington, DC. "Ironic though," N. said, "because Paul is a French company and LavAzza is Italian." But N. and I were not here to discuss artisan coffee or the ironies of the world. Unless the explosion of an entire town could be considered ironic.

"We think there were only a few dozen residents," N. explained, "and we have reason to believe these individuals were a unique breed of homosapien." I watched N. sip the cup of coffee tentatively, the heat steaming from the top of the mug. Sitting there, I betrayed no emotion. I could already tell that N. was the type of source who would continue talking if I kept quiet. "We've been studying remains for weeks now, but it's all very hush hush. And the entire investigation is compartmentalized. I know very little and that is intentional."

I asked N. about the photographs. "I'm not even allowed to mention them," N. said. "No one on my team is permitted to discuss the pictures. Which of course means there must be some truth to them." I was shocked when I heard this. It seemed hardly possible that those rows of glass houses sitting peacefully in a clearing in the woods, the circular walkways surrounding what might be a town square, the larger buildings in the distance that could be warehouses—how could those have remained hidden in the North Carolina countryside? "It's a question we can't ask," N. told me.

All of the reporting to date has suggested that the photographs are a hoax. But digital experts have been flummoxed by the variability of the images, how sometimes the pictures depict a wide expanse of woods—a sea of trees—while a second glance might reveal, if only for a handful of seconds, a small but contemporary-looking village within the forest. "It's technology that we are not yet familiar with. We cannot yet say how they are able to alter their images," an FBI analyst told me a few days after my meeting with N.

Back in Connelly Springs, I visited a town hall meeting one Tuesday evening. I sat behind Phillip in a folding chair with rusting legs that rested unevenly on the old wood floor. "We need answers," someone in the front shouted. A chorus of approval swept through the close, hot air in the room. "My husband been missin' since the explosion," cried a woman a few rows in front of me, wearing a bright yellow hat that covered most of her gray hair.

Next, I saw JD stand up, his body almost as large and imposing as his voice: "We got the CIA here, the FBI, the NSA, the XYZ, and all them other letters combined—and they aint' tellin' us shit! They got nearly a hundred acres of land cordoned off, and they tellin's us we can't do a thing about it!" He paused to catch his breath, his arms gesticulating wildly about him, the entire room's attention fixed upon him. "Phillip's parents is dead! Mrs. Jones' husband is missin' along with the entire Franklin family! We cannot stand by and watch the government cover this up!" There were shouts in the room. Nearly everyone had stood to their feet, save for those in wheelchairs and myself, holding onto my mini shotgun mic and furiously taking notes.

Soon, the entire town, it seemed, was marching through the woods, following the creek behind JD's Smokehouse. I joined them with hesitation. As a journalist, I cannot commit any illegal acts during the course of my reporting. That Tuesday evening, following the locals through the dense forest, I had no idea whose land we were on, whether

we were trespassing, or worse—whether we had breached the perimeter that government officials had set up around the explosion site.

The woods became more dense as we walked. The path we took had faded into the detritus of the forest ground: leaves still wet from a recent summer rain, twigs snapping beneath our feet, and—the further we walked—mounds of freshly charred earth. We all stopped short when a small clearing in the trees revealed a high, chain-link fence topped with circular loops of razors like those enclosing the many prisons and correctional facilities I knew were scattered across this rural, North Carolina landscape. What I observed next, after a few of the men used pliers to cut away at the fence, has been omitted from this article simply because it cannot be fact-checked.

A few weeks later, my fact-checker and I met with another government official in DC. This particular source had somewhat elaborate requirements for our meeting: she instructed us to wear "tourist" clothes (I purchased a "USA" hoodie and a selfie-stick at one of the street vendors) and to meet her inside of the Smithsonian Castle. She tapped me on my shoulder as I was examining the crypt of James Smithson.

We strolled through the intricate Enid A. Haupt Garden, the sun glaring down upon us. "There appears to be some kind of invisible barrier," she told me, "I can show you a picture."

My fact-checker and I watched as she produced an iPad from her bag. The picture appeared normal at first: only dense trees, similar to the ones I'd walked through back in Connelly Springs. But then, quicker than a blink of the eye, the long-half of a body appeared on the screen: a man's left hand and leg (I could see the hairs on his arm, the simple leather wristwatch, the rolled-up cuff of a dress shirt), but the other half of him was invisible, as though it had slipped into another dimension.

And then she showed us another photo. This picture did not change its image. It appeared static. It was a photo of a sign, and this is what it read: Welcome to Desperate, population, 100. ◆

The Lost Letters of Catherine Frances
Collected by Elyse Rudemiller, Archival Team Member

Welcome to Room #2 of our tour through the Lost Colony of Desperate.
While there are many profoundly useful discoveries in our exhibition that
illuminate the mystery of Desperate, North Carolina, firstly, we in the special collections divisions must proudly present authenticated letter fragments
from Agathe Alami, née Gifford, to her sister Catherine Francis, née Gifford.
These letters, donated by the estate of the Francis' family, upon discovery of
our archival work here at the university, have proven to be invaluable in the
parsing of Desperate's true origins.

While the archival team has been hard at work to decipher these corre-
spondences, as in all archival work, there are some sections that have become
lost to time, having grown truly undecipherable, or are otherwise irrecov-
erable. As such, the archival team has taken some creative liberties to fill in
the blanks where appropriate based on the expertise of resident linguist and
Desperate expert, Professor Cadwell Turnbull, who has been an integral con-
sultant and leader in the construction of The Lost Colony of Desperate: The
Interactive Exhibition.

Now, if you would please be seated, as the first portion of this room involves a brief holo-dramatic reenactment of sections of the letter fragments
below. Also, be forewarned that because of the nature of virtual reality, these
scenes are immersive and can be disorienting for some viewers. You should
also be aware that there are some violent or disturbing images. If you find
either of these things concerning, you may opt out of the presentation by
moving forward through the exhibit. We are immensely grateful to The Royal
Theater, whose acting company we proudly partner with here at The Lost
Colony of Desperate, and whose talented day players have starred in many
of our interactive exhibitions, such as last fall's exhibition detailing the failed

presidency of international war criminal Donald Trump. For regular updates about museum offerings, please be sure to subscribe to our virtual mailing lists.

We hope you enjoyed the presentation. Now, please proceed forward and enjoy "The Lost Letters of Catherine Francis."

THE LOST LETTERS OF CATHERINE FRANCES

Excerpted letters from colony member Agathe Alami, née Gifford, to her sister Catherine Frances, née Gifford. Generously donated from the estate of the Frances family.

January 19, '25

Catherine,

I know my time is drawing close and, dare I say it, I am afraid. There is no midwife in our new settlement. We have a neighbor-woman, Old Franny, who said she would help with the birth, but even that knowledge isn't enough to stay the dread. It feels like just moments ago we watched our dear sister cradling our niece on those blood-soaked sheets. Do you think we did wrong? Letting the babe stay there until her body had grown cold? My stomach turns when I think of it, trying in vain to suckle at her breast, and wailing to find it cold and empty.

Osman says not to be afraid, that Charlotte's affliction will not be mine, but that is a man's attitude. They don't know—haven't lived with the knowledge from the time they're little children—that when they have children, they may die. He tells me I'm brave. He tells me that I wouldn't have left, have come to this new world with him, if I wasn't. I just nod when he says such things. I want to tell him that death doesn't care whether I'm brave or not.

And yet, I know if I was brave. I wouldn't have left. I would have stayed with you and helped fill the space left by Charlotte's absence, but I couldn't bear it. Forgive me sister, and forgive me my silliness. I'm sure all will be well. I'll write again when the babe is born.

–Agathe

February, 22 '25

Catherine,

Well, it is done. The pain was near unbearable—at times I felt I might be ripped in two. Did you feel that way when yours were born? Old Franny held my hand and wiped the sweat from my neck. Although she tried to hide it, I could see the fear in her eyes. She had a small boy go and fetch Osman to my side although I was naked and wild and gasping. That's when

I became truly afraid. Osman held me still while Franny reached inside of me and twisted the infant. When she instructed me to, I pushed and pushed and pushed. At times it felt like I was pushing out part of myself and not the child. Finally, exhausted, I bore down one last time. I felt that I was splitting, like the skin of a ripe plum. I screamed. Then came immeasurable relief, pinpricks of starlight behind my eyelids, and finally, darkness.

The strangest thing happened next, dear sister. When I awoke, I was trapped in a sheet, the fragrant scent of lavender tucked next to my face. I panicked and desperately worked to untangle myself. When I managed to pull myself free, in the dim light of the fire, I saw that my body had been washed and sweet herbs pressed into my skin. Franny and Osman stared at me then, frozen and fearful until Osman sprang to me, tears rolling down his cheeks. He clutched me, the little bundle of our babe between us. He told me that they thought I had died. His skin was near feverish next to mine. We embraced until panic overcame me, and I snatched the quiet roll that he held into my own. What of the child? Surely if it was living, I would hear its cry. My heart slowed and I wept when I saw the babe's cheeks were ruddy with life.

We have a son, my dear sister. He is fat and perfect, and like his first few hours on this earth, never cries. Yet sometimes, when I look into his dark eyes, there is a tick of sadness I cannot place.

–Agathe

March 29, '30

Catherine,

William is nigh on five years now. He's a sweet boy with hair dark as rich soil. Osman and I have tried to conceive again, but have had no success. Perhaps there was too much damage from William's birth. I'm afraid he will be my only child. Nevertheless, our lives are mostly content. Peaceful. But although we never whispered a word of what happened that night, I can see the glances of suspicion when I walk about town.

In truth, I'm not the only one about whom the town whispers. A few years back John Sambutima was caught under a felled tree. His wife found him, limp and lifeless, crushed under the great trunk. But when a party was arranged to pull the tree off, his eyes fluttered open and he sprang up as if he'd just awoken for the day. And just last month, the Valencia's twins went missing and didn't appear until three weeks later when the last of the winter thaw cracked the ice on the lake. They showed up purple and shivering and said they'd fallen in. Despite all our questioning, they couldn't recall where they'd been in the weeks between then and now.

Slight things those children are, you'd hardly know they were years older than their younger sister. Don't seem to have grown at all since our arrival. There have been some lean winters though—perhaps they're not getting enough to eat. Next week I think I'll take the Valencias some apples from our tree. William is growing as quickly as a wild grape vine. I'm forever letting out the seams of his clothing.

Do consider coming, sister. It would be a joy to have you visit. Although travelers have brought us news of tragedy from other colonies—sickness and starvation—we've had no such ill-luck. In fact, we've lost not one man, woman, or child, since we've arrived. Even Old Franny is still with us, though her face was pruned as a peach pit before we even stepped ashore. I suppose a few have lost babes in the womb, but all of us who came together stand strong. I just thank God that William is still healthy and hearty as ever.

April 24, '33

Catherine,

I was sorry to hear of mother's death. It has kept me up many nights these last few months. I'm troubled that I was unable to be there with her in the end—although sometimes I'm grateful too. If I could escape bearing witness to the deaths of any more of those I love—I think I would—to never lose the image of them as happy and vital, just as they were in their lives.

In that respect we've been lucky. Most of us are as sturdy as we were the day we stepped off the ship... oddly so. For all the hardship my hands have endured in this place: scraping at rocky earth, blistering under the harvest sun, peeling from the strong lye I use to wash—they still seem as soft and supple as the day we landed. Of course, we've no mirror, but Osman tells me I look just the picture of the girl he married. I can't tell if he's just being mannerly, but either way, I suppose I should be grateful. I've either a good man, a healthy constitution, or both. He looks ever youthful, himself. There must be something to all this fresh air.

–Agathe

September 16, '34

Catherine,

There is surely something strange going on here. For many years, I simply thought us lucky... but all the deaths that turned out not to be... and the children that do not seem to grow... it pesters my mind like a gnat next to the ear. There were few children that made it through the journey here, but the handful that did are showing no signs of growing older. Perhaps I'd be able to ignore it, but the children that were born on this soil are beginning to look more aged than those who stepped aground with us.

Ourselves too, Catherine, none of us seem much changed. I know there are others amongst us, who whisper about it behind closed doors, but we are–all of us–too scared to discuss it openly I think.

Perhaps it is just the imagination. A trick of this place, played on us by the fresh air and sunshine. Maybe the children born on this patch of earth just have stronger constitutions. Afterall, there were many hardships here to get used to: hard farm labor, swarms of buzzing mosquitoes, stifling summers. Perhaps they have just been built more solidly to account for it. But still, I think it cannot be. A man came through, not long ago, and sold the Ansomas a looking glass. We've all taken turns looking in it, and sister, when I peered in I expected to see an older woman. Maybe a faint veining of wrinkles, or a gentle sag of the jaw, but the girl I saw in front of me was bright eyed and fresh faced. I daren't complain about possessing youth, but it's almost as if the years here haven't even happened.

–Agathe

May 10, '35

Catherine,

I'm sending this before you've even gotten the last letter, but things have gotten ever stranger here. Three nights ago, Mr. Ming—you know, the one I told you that joined this endeavor to pay off his debts—he had a disagreement with a stranger passing through and aimed to settle it with a duel. They had both quite set their minds on it, there was nothing to be done other than to let them resolve the dispute. A crowd of us followed them to a clearing at the edge of the wood. At the count of ten, they both shot and fell to the ground. One of their bullets must have bounced off or through the intended target, because the preacher fell as well.

We were all in a terror. The stranger lay unmoving, clutching at his chest.

Mr. Ming—it was a sight—a portion of his skull lay in the dirt, a slick of pink brain exposed, while the preacher clutched at his gut. I wish I could unsee... I looked too long and saw a slippery piece of organ escaping his belly, shining in the sun. The physician rushed to help them, though it was clear that nothing could be done. She placed the piece of skull back and pushed in the gut, but didn't bother to take out her tools. The families were called to come collect the bodies. Just as they arrived, running with flushed faces—the preacher and Mr. Ming began to stir. It was like watching one of those old puppet shows we used to stop and watch in the square. Do you remember those? Little wooden puppets with strings attached to their limbs that jerked them around as if they were living souls. Well, it was like that. Our men rose up as if something controlled them, while the stranger lay still in the dirt.

The physician examined our men once more, and though blood still stained their clothing, she could find no marks on their bodies. If it was the work of God or the Devil, I cannot be sure. Perhaps because it was the preacher, we can say that it was God. There have been no cries of witchcraft, for which I am grateful. We don't need to war amongst ourselves. Perhaps, too, because if we begin accusing others, it won't be long before we are the accused ourselves. It seems that there has been at least one occurrence in each family in which someone should have died—but didn't. Sometimes, when I wake up in a tangle of sheets, or smell the sweet split buds of fresh lavender, my palms begin to sweat and I feel that I am still in my death shroud.

I think that maybe I really did die that night. The night William was born. Maybe the whole town has died and we just don't know yet that we're already in the afterlife. If that is so, it's certainly not the afterlife that was promised.

–Agathe

Last letter never postmarked, found among the belongings of Agathe and Osman Alami.

December 19, '70

Catherine,

I'm sorry it's been so long since I've written. I think of you often and miss you more often than that. Since that day I wrote you so long ago, when we saw Mr. Ming and the preacher raise back to life, much has changed. So much has happened. One of our young men went to the seaside to trade, and was killed in a brawl. When he raised back to life, it was strangers eyes upon him, not our own. He was immediately taken for a witch or a demon, and they devised all manners of evil to try to rid this earth of him: hanging, burning, pressing. After the night they tried to burn him, he feigned death long enough to make his escape. Eventually making his way back. When he told us what he endured, we knew we weren't safe in the world. Although it seems that we can't die, we feel the same pain. And those that fear us would inflict it upon us again and again.

Since that day, we have limited our doings with those beyond our borders. We stopped sending mail, we no longer married outsiders, we traded infrequently and, even then, never disclosed from where we'd come. There were a few settlements in the area that already knew we were here though, and we couldn't erase ourselves from their memories. People came on occasion to trade or stop for the night. Eventually the day that we all feared came. A traveler came through who disappeared in the night, taking with them Lillian Rumstead and her children. We worried, but hoped for the best at first. Lillian's husband had long been unkind to her. I, personally, was happy that she'd been able to get away. There were many occasions on which she'd shown up on the doorstep of another family and passed the night there. But Lillian wasn't originally one of us, she was an outsider. The Rumsteads met after we'd arrived and married once we settled—before we knew. As the years passed, the Rumsteads began to look more like mother and son than wife and husband.

I think perhaps if Mr. Rumstead had been more favorable to his wife, what happened next mightn't have occurred. She'd been gone for some few weeks, when a mob appeared in the night, carrying torches that lept like hell flames. They shouted at us, shrieking that we were abominations, demons, a scourge. That surely, if we lived that meant that somewhere else, others died. She must have shared our secret. I can hardly blame her, we should have given her more kindness here. They burned down our buildings and when we emerged, screaming in the night, they took to us with muskets, hatchets, whatever they had. I looked into the eyes of the man who put a pitchfork through my belly, his eyes blazed with righteousness. When he was done with me, he moved on. They killed every last soul.

When they had finished their work, shrouded by smoke, they gathered together and prayed. The joined hands as a preacher sprinkled holy water on the ground and said a blessing. I watched them, gasping on the ground, as my heart quietly emptied my body of blood. After they finished their prayer, they ransacked what little remained, and added pitch to the blazes, to ensure that we would burn.

It didn't work. When I awoke, my clothing was melted to my skin. We weren't so lucky as to get to die. Well, most of us. We had long since suspected that the children we bore here did not share this same power, this affliction. Afterall, we could see them age when we did not. William, my sweet boy, was by then a man of twenty-five. He'd just settled with the Valencia girl. It was luck really, that they were both born here and so close in age. So many of our children have had no partners from whom to choose. I'm glad he had some happiness at least. I found their bodies myself. They were outside, corpses clutched to each other, feet away from the husk of their burned home. We collected and buried our dead. It was a ghoulish scene. People still dressed in their bloody and burnt clothing. We didn't have to ask one other what death they had endured, the evidence of it still on our bodies. We dug graves. The first we had needed. Even children worked, helping to bury the adult bodies of their younger siblings.

It was then that a meeting of the town council was convened. We knew the world—people—were too dangerous. We could neither go into the outside world, nor let it come to us. We rebuilt. We constructed trails that led in wide circles around our border and blocked the paths that led to our gates, letting them become overgrown and hidden by new life. And here, hidden from the world, we remain.

I know we are unlike to meet again, sister. Just as I know that I will never send this letter. I supposed I will outlive you, and your children, and their children too—although the reason for this is still not clear. We here are bound to live out our considerable days, right here in this spot. And still, I cannot make up my mind about it. It seems such a blessing to be unable to die, but yet, if so–why does it feel like a curse?

–Agathe

The Corporeal Peculiarity of Desperate Citizenry

Collected by Jendayi Brooks-Flemister,
Archival Team Member

Welcome to Room #3 on our tour through the Lost Colony of Desperate. Here we will dive into the strange medical maladies of Desperate citizenry, observed and recorded by Desperate physicians. These records, painstakingly exhumed by archeologist Jendayi Brooks-Flemister, have helped immensely in understanding the nature of what it meant to be a member of the Desperate community. Though many questions still remain unanswered, these documents provide valuable insight into how the people of Desperate coped with the realization of who they were and what that truth would mean for their future.

Please be on the lookout for additional reenactments by The Royal Theater. For our younger guests or those squeamish to blood, we would advise that you bypass the virtual surgical diorama in Booth #3, which contains graphic images not suitable to sensitive viewers. Now, please proceed clockwise around the room to chronologically follow the physician's logs of Desperate.

THE CORPOREAL PECULIARITY
OF DESPERATE CITIZENRY

A small journal was among many other artifacts recovered from the explosion. Parts of the journal have been transcribed from the original handwriting below. – Jendayi Brooks-Flemister

Herein shall reside all records of the Physician's observations, patients' information, and, whereupon necessary, the Physician's imminent thoughts and understandings of the town of Desperate's residents, including, but not limited to, the seemingly immortal afflictions of said residents.

July 1, '35

Due to being present for the disagreement, I, Lily Everstone, have been chosen by the town council as the town's first official Physician. While I must say that I am honored by the opportunity to serve the town of Desperate fully, I must admit that my knowledge of how Mr. Ming and the Preacher found themselves contorting back into their beings without warning is limited. It was a horrific sight, but one that I have promised to study to comprehend the phenomenon. I shall record my thoughts on my findings dutifully in this journal, though I shall keep my actual research in a separate Physician's Log. L.E.

October 22, '35

Upon extensive interviewing with the town's 100 permanent residents, I have come to the conclusion that we are all, in the loosest sense of the word, immortal from our current ages. There has been no one, besides the Preacher, who has any understanding of what may have triggered such a pulse of immortality amongst us. To our knowledge, we and our offspring are unable to die, or rather, to remain dead. No matter the physical affliction to our bodies, our bones and organs and veins twist and puppeteer themselves back together. As those who have "died" have said, it is like taking a short nap and waking up in a startled confusion.

I spent a great deal of time studying Mr. Ming, as his death has remained the most gruesome I have witnessed or heard of. He could not explain any unnatural feeling of something rising or twisting within him, no call from a higher being, no life force flowing outward or inward. It was absolutely not of his will, nor the Preacher's, nor any other resident's will, to return to this existence. I am becoming increasingly determined to understand just what this means for us all. L.E.

November 3, '35

That fool Isaiah Patters set himself aflame as a testing joke to his own ability to resurrect. I and several others warned him, but Mr. Ming jokingly asserted that a full-bodied death would be a most gruesome recovery. Isaiah set himself aflame with their shared bottle of whiskey in the center of town. It was a most horrific scene–his laughs turned to screams as every inch of him charred. The smell was horrendous–many of us regrettably lost our lunch. Levi and Esther doused him with water as soon as they could, but the fool died from the severity of the heat. As I examined his body in my office, his skin regrew within minutes before my very eyes. I had hardly touched him. When he came to just a few minutes afterward, his only question for me was to know how it looked when he set himself aflame. He walked out of my office to go finish the whiskey with Mr. Ming before I could respond. Perhaps I, too, need a drink. L.E.

Dec 30, '35

As it has grown too cold to conduct outside research further, I have to cease my research and reflect upon my current findings. To my knowledge, based on my gatherings from the townspeople, there is still no basis for our assumed immortality. We do not eat the same things, some of us drink from different streams. We cannot be sure what has caused us to be this way. At this point, it feels hopeless. The children, such as little Gertie, seem to be incapable of puberty. Were I able to understand the intricacies of their minds, I might study how this affects them. Alas, I have instead resolved myself to tending to the pregnant and aiding with small coughs as they arise. L.E.

February 7, '40

There is little to record upon knowing now that whatever our affliction, we are still here. The town has built itself up quite nicely. Our council will hold elections and nominations this year, to which I am hoping to become part of. While I appreciate being appointed the Physician, I am especially bored of the ever-present wailing of babies as several of us from town find partners from other areas. The babies do not seem afflicted with anything that would indicate that they, too, are incapable of permanent death. So as more babies have come, I have found myself neglecting this position more and more. The only so-called illness I am tending is, unfortunately, the fool Isaiah and his need to scare us all with lighting himself aflame every now and then. I am hopeful that as a councilmember, I will be able to restrict his proximity to matches. L.E.

March 15, '40

Due to council election, I, Wilhelmina Trout, have taken on the responsibility of being the town's Physician. I have only done so as a favor to Lily, who is now a councilmember and to whom I have been acquainted with for years. I have seen to it that there are term limits placed upon the role of Physician, a minimum of five and maximum of twenty years, so that no one is stuck in this boring role for long. W.T.

Mar 15, '45

Due to council election, I, Samuel Trout, have taken on the responsibility of being the town's Physician. S.T.

Dec 31, '55

There are quite a few children who, as far as we can tell, have not physically aged in decades. As of now, we have had seven children born amongst the town. Four have been born within the past two years. They are all healthy, which has prompted many of us to wonder at what age the children will cease aging and begin their immortality phase. I have no answer, though I worry that there will be many ten-year-olds running around for eternity if they acquire immortality too soon. There is only so much we can do for them. S.T.

Nov 29, '63

We learned this week that the children are not immortal, as we'd believed before. Agatha's boy, William, was murdered during the Attack. I am terrified to know what this means for us as a colony, as a town. Our future depends on our children, or so we had all primitively assumed. With this understanding, I have had the two expectant mothers kill themselves so that the baby they carried would die inside of them. I have had to perform the operation, both times, to take the dead embryos out. This has sparked a new fear that we never knew we should have. And with the council's decision that Desperate shall henceforth remain separate from the outside world for our own protection, we are now more aware of our own lack of mortality than ever. Is this what I have resigned myself to? Am I destined to pull unborn fetuses from pregnant women for as long as I remain Physician? I cannot. Wilhelmina and I have a little one. Will we outlive her? Can we give her what we have? I am working with Lily's research, and so far, nothing has proven to me that we shall see our daughter last longer than we will. S.T.

Mar 12, '68
  I have been reelected for the time being. Wilhelmina is pregnant again. After talking with August and the Preacher, we have decided to keep our child. S.T.

Mar 15, '90
  Due to council election, I, Tati Sena, have taken on the responsibility of being the town's Physician. I am not trained in much. T.S.

May 14, '93
  Today I was told by the council that I should not suggest people drown themselves to get rid of a cough. I did not know I could not do this. T.S.

February 26, '96
  Today there was a small bout of diarrhea amongst several townsfolk after ingesting a poorly treated piece of rabbit jerky. When the townsfolk asked for my assistance, I told them that I also was afflicted and could not help them. Perhaps this job is not for me. T.S.

June 7, '04
  There is so little to do as Physician. I have resigned myself to using Isaiah as a way to test out new medicines. So far nothing seems to matter, though. If I mistakenly give him a medicinal treatment that could kill him, he willingly dies and comes back asking for another round. All I have learned is that we can, so far as I am able to tell, die and resurrect an innumerable amount of times. Which, I must admit, now that there are so few pregnancies, has become quite the nuisance. T.S.

Mar 15, '18

Due to council election, I, Essi Lane, have taken on the responsibility of being the town's Physician. I will thoroughly admit within the confines of this journal that it has been years since an illness of "life-threatening" proportions. Our life is confined to this town, to drinking from the river and harvesting from forests and building farms nearby. We have no knowledge of the outside world due to the outside world's rejection of us. Perhaps one day we will find a way to change our fate. For now, I shall maintain records of possible remedies to our ailment. E.L.

Archivist Note: All remaining entries from the journal are unfortunately too damaged to be transcribed, but our archival staff is working diligently on future excavations of currently illegible documents, and should any new discoveries occur, they will be promptly announced and added to our exhibition.

Behind the Lens

*Collected by Isaac Hughes Green,
Archival Team Member*

Welcome to Room #4 on our tour through the Lost Colony of Desperate.
What follows is an article detailing the harrowing adventure and obses-
sions of Axel Herzog, grandson to Werner Herzog, who noticed something
strange about a photograph of Desperate after a near-death experience in
the Bavarian Alps, just as his grandfather Werner once had. Axel was among
a handful of people who nearly witnessed the wonder of seeing a Desperate
photo for what it truly is. As a member of the Herzog family, widely known
for its eccentric members, the piece was initially panned by critics and de-
rided as fake. It wasn't until recent years that interest in it was renewed and,
having lived a short, tumultuous life, Axel Herzog was posthumously nom-
inated for a Pulitzer Prize.

Please be sure to check our holographic Herzog key chains available for
purchase at our gift shop. A special thanks to the Herzog estate for their
cooperation with our exhibition.

You may now proceed forward. The document is displayed in the center
of the room—but you will also find the text projected onto the walls for
easier reading. Video of early interviews of Herzog discussing his discovery
can also be found throughout the exhibit.

Hey Sean,

This is the draft of the article that hack wrote. If you ask me, it belongs on the History channel superimposed on one of those shows they broadcast about how the pyramids came from aliens. But hey... He's a Herzog... And if there's one thing the industry is good for, it's keeping nepotism alive. Just put it in between camera breakdowns of two movies nobody cares about and call it a day.

Yours,
Isaac
—

ISAAC GREEN
MANAGING EDITOR – AMERICAN CINEMATOGRAPHER
CINEMATOGRAPHER (ASC)
HOLLYWOOD, CA
(***) ***_****

"The Heart and The Photograph"
By Axel Herzog

Where does a photograph begin and where does it end? Our modern conceptions of photography tell us that the medium on which the photograph is printed is where it starts and ends. It is a two-dimensional rendering according to convention, only jutting out into reality at the atomic level, where dektol or celluloid or some combination of the two make it tangible and allow it to have dynamic range which gives us what we see.

And based on the history of photography, the way it has been taught over the years, you might think that this is all there is to a photograph. We, as the image-making community, understand that the theory of optics on which modern photography is based came from Ibn al-Haytham who, in the early 11th century, claimed to be able to regulate the flooding of the Nile and, upon failure to do so, was locked into his home without access to food or water. There he observed rays of light entering through a small window and creating an image against a wall. It was a flat wall and the image he observed is understood to have been just that, a flat image, with no connection to anything but the objects outside of the window that scattered the light in order to create it. The camera obscura that Joseph Niepce used to create the first tactile photographic image some seven hundred years later is contemporarily understood in a similar way. He used asphalt which was light sensitive to create a rendering of an image and called it heliography or "drawing with the sun". Even my grandfather, Werner Herzog, is understood to have been an artist who directed and acted in a three-dimensional space but, created films that were solely experienceable in two dimensions. But what if there were more to their discoveries?

With the advent of virtual reality and 3D technology, we've been able to experience images reaching out to us—dinosaurs flying out of screens and into theaters, car crashes exploding at the tips of our noses, waves of water bringing us down into the depths of oceans. But what if there were another dimension to image making and imagery that were waiting to be unlocked and lay dormant until viewed in the right set of circumstances?

Before I reveal to you my discovery, you must understand how strange and incomprehensible the discoveries made in photography have each seemed when they were revealed to the general public. In antiquity, before Ibn al-Haytham, the generally accepted theories on vision were that the eyes were either emitting rays of light or were being entered by physical objects which allowed humanity to see. Al-Haytham must have been thought to be a heretic when he theorized that light itself was not a physical object, but a ray, which was not being emitted, but was entering the eye in a straight line.

Sure, there were forms of lithography around the time that Joseph Niepce created his first photograph. Artisans carved from wood and other materials and created images which were reprinted. But imagine him telling a neighbor that his rendering was caused by the sun. It would be a moment parallel to one of Jesus' miracles and was probably perceived as such.

I don't need to remind you of the magic of movies because you've already experienced them, no doubt. But maybe taking you back to the reactions of the first movie theater goers will remind you of how revolutionary the moving picture was. The first moviegoers saw a coming train depicted on a screen and ducked in their seats or ran out of the theater for fear they'd be flattened. If that isn't a testament to the fact that advances in imaging technology are often imperceptible to those that haven't been exposed them, then I don't know what is.

With that in mind, I'd like to tell you a story. I did a lot of soul searching in my youth and always felt like I was floating through life—disconnected. I dabbled in drugs and art and all of the things you try when you don't want people to forget you exist. And then I wanted to experience something real. That led me to my grandfather's homeland of Bavaria. I wanted to experience what he'd experienced—the remote mountains that had given him his detached and measured perspective, which he'd become so famous for.

I wasn't as patient as I should have been. Sure, the Chiemgau Alps in Bavaria that my Grandfather grew up within are only a third as tall as mountains like K2 or Everest. But that doesn't mean you can strap on a pair of hiking boots overtop your acid washed jeans and climb up like it was Runyon Canyon. Even though people had told me I needed to prepare I went hastily. I was alone. And as I summited I felt the cold and the hypoxia. I could feel my body giving way. I laid in the snow and stared up at the pale blue sky—hoping the villagers I'd briefly encountered would come up and try to find me if I passed out or wasn't able to make my way back down. And I felt like I was close to death. My heart never stopped. My eyes were always open. But I began to imagine what it would be like to no longer be there anymore. Maybe it was because I was all alone in the wilderness. Maybe death just sounds like a whipping wind over a mountain crest peak—feels like the blood slowing down in your veins as the ice causes it to thicken. I'll never know until it's time. For now, what I know for certain is that I didn't die or even lose consciousness. But I came close.

As I regained my strength, I made my way back down and stayed where my grandfather had stayed. I was warmed up by a fire and fed soup and bread. And then I came back to L.A. and resumed my life as a trust fund kid whose sole public facing enterprise was when I participated in the legacy I'd been left. But, I wanted to be more. I wanted a way into my grandfather's industry that I could carve out myself—to get my name out there for something I did. I just needed to figure out what that thing was.

I combed through old movies and tried to pick out ones that I could come up with an original take on. And then I tried to learn about cameras and invent new accessories that would make life easier for the overworked assistants and runners. Finally, I came upon a photograph in a museum. It was said to be of a place called Desperate. But, no one that looked at the photograph was able to see the city hidden within. Only the photographer and the museum curator who'd taken the photograph into his collection had ever been recorded as seeing the city. And I wondered if there could be some technological trick I could perform to unearth the image that was hidden to the masses.

I had what was left of the money from grandfather at my disposal and I tried everything from electron microscopes to alternative processing of the negative. At first it was a hobby, but it became an obsession. I burned through my inheritance searching for Desperate and came up short until I was running out of money for food and rent. I had the photograph with me—on loan from the museum – and was laying in my bed one night, wondering if I should scrape together pennies to go to the store and buy a meal. I looked up at the ceiling and was reminded of when I'd been on my back at the top of the mountain. Without having eaten in days, I felt the cold wash over me. The white paint in my apartment looked blue for a moment—like the sky had been that day. And then I looked at the photograph (pictured above), while still feeling the way I'd felt. That was when I saw it. Little buildings and trails of smoke from fires in each of them. It went away a few seconds later, once the feeling had faded. And I couldn't see it again when I tried to conjure it back. But there was no denying what I'd seen. And no denying that it had been connected to how I'd felt.

So, I write this article to ask you—what if there were a dimension to photography beyond the physical? What if our feelings determined how we see images? What if our feelings when composing images determined how they would or could be perceived by later viewers? Wasn't Ibn Al-Haythem at death's door barricaded in his home with no access to outside food or water when he laid the groundwork for the photograph? Couldn't Niepce have been similarly destitute? I know for a fact that my grandfather was. Perhaps they could have seen what they saw because of what was in the physical world around them. But what if it was the feelings they'd had that had allowed them their prescient revelations?

I don't know how the technology works. All I know is that what I saw was real.

The Verses of Desperate

Collected by Misha Lazzara, Archival Team Member

Welcome to Room #5 on our tour through the Lost Colony of Desperate.
Desperate Archivist, Misha Lazzara, has worked tirelessly to bring fragmented findings of poetry, badly damaged in the infamous explosion that destroyed nearly all of life in Desperate, here to you all. As such, you will note that certain poems are missing words, or have been recreated with the best attempts, in coordination with our graphology division.

It is quite important to note for our guests that the historical importance of the content found in Cherry's poems has shifted with time. These poems have been highly debated amongst modern scholars and their meaning has grown in tandem with our modern understanding of what exactly occurred near Desperate's end. What do you believe, dear guest? What do the poems of Cherry illuminate about Desperate for you?

Please be seated for a virtual reality reenactment by The Royal Company of portions of the poems displayed in the exhibit. The dramatization of these poems involves a discussion of sexuality, which may not be appropriate for children. As always, if you do not wish to view the reenactment, you may simply proceed forward into the exhibit.

Once you've viewed the poetry of Cherry brought to life by The Royal Theater, please enter the exhibit and enjoy the original documents. You will also find email correspondence from the archivist herself, detailing Lazzara's thoughts concerning the poems.

As you will see, even scholars have debated the identity of the poet and the nature of her poetry. As you make your way through the exhibit, keep that in mind. Who do you think Cherry is? What do you think some of the illegible words might be?

Sarah,

Here are scans of the leather-bound collection of poetry located at the site of the explosion (that I promised to send six months ago). Today was our cutoff date, but the head of dept. still might give me grief for sending now. We were instructed to keep it close for as long as we could. The poems are fascinating, but I didn't see a lot of artistic progression from the first to the last. Maybe there was limited exposure to new art forms in their settlement, especially the generations after the raid. Likely wasn't a poet laureate among the first group of settlers, though it's hard to make sense of the disparate news emerging on who the settlers were (initially). "Cherry" is the only name we have for her—likely a pen name (maybe a pet name or nickname). I don't have much access to anything beyond the manifest, but two young women—Estye and Naomi—are likely candidates as far as static age. I'm sure more information will be released as data is compiled.

Damage to top right corner: singe marks, smoke damage, and words cut off. Also, certain words were illegible on the pages even without damage, creating a deeper enigma in all of this. Language examined by literature and language scholars here at NCSU and a much larger cohort of visiting experts, including various period experts spanning medieval, Romantic, modern as well as language historian E.B. Bower. Everyone is arguing that the work fits in with only their period (everyone wants their hands on this). Notes and annotations included for your review. This collection isn't going anywhere, but you better be grateful. There will be so many articles and essays about this—and fast. Maybe a movie deal too, eventually. Though I'm not sure who they could cast as the girl, considering the age issue. Maybe it would be too weird for viewers to process, in the end. I'm sorry these are out of order. I would get a TA to go through the scans to match the pages in the book, but I can't have it getting out that I'm sending them so soon.

I visited the museum with the photograph, too. Couldn't see anything but a river, some trees—just like you said. Maybe we're not Desperate enough. Ha—dumb joke. Give my regards to Beth.

Best,
ML

Stanzas

Cast the first stone if you will.
Before you do, please ask yourself:
How long must a girl stay a child
and never become a woman?

I only watch my own reflection.
Some dark magic and all these glass walls
keep us hidden from the world.
Always a maiden, never a maid.

I asked him to toss the granite
ever so gently, a simple shattering
but he feared my soft curls
and my bare garden.

[Note: Most of Cherry's early poems explore yearning, a girl on the brink of sexuality. Interesting to note that she is not naïve or bright-eyed about men, sexuality or romantic love. Perhaps these poems are nostalgic or recall her past, a past as some kind of perpetual virgin. We posit that there are potential manuscripts similar to but predating this one—leather-bound, handmade from cowhide and pulped bark—that have been lost. If so, it's possible the poet could have been any "age" here—a "woman" in her forties, fifties or potentially one-hundred-and-fifties. We have no idea. There are no dates. Of course, later poems lead us to believe she found a partner, had a child, experienced sexual relationships. —M. Matthews.]

Stanza

We stopped celebrating new moons
New years faded into dust
My mother and I bleed together now
Forever our monthlies run red
Moon after moon after
On that maiden voyage I was a maiden still

For many years they insisted
I was too young to be a bride
Perhaps not yet fifteen, perhaps twenty-five
Then thirty, forty, we stopped noticing seasons
I was the only one left to notice
I would never become a woman
Study, they said, so rare an opportunity for a girl
Labor, they offered, as if that would replace
A man between my legs
[Illegible] they scoffed at my bawdy, tawdry
Desperate desires
Eventually, I stopped begging
And discovered that crack in the glass

[Later poems reveal Cherry's pregnancy and the subsequent death of her child in the raids. We note she is perhaps fourteen, but not precise. Unsure if she predates a time when people were fully able to track birthdays, had forgotten it by this time in her life, or if it was a custom of class and culture not to track or have education to track the exact date of birth.

The poetic form is surprisingly free—almost modern—but without dates, we're not clear when she started writing poetry or when she stopped. It's certainly not metered nor Romantic, as she almost never discusses the landscape or nature, never rhymes or counts syllables, at least in this manuscript. We surmise that after witnessing a potentially unfathomable number of sunrises, it's possible Cherry stopped engaging with the notion of pastoral beauty. Regardless, there is certainly a focus on repressed or frustrated sexuality. One idea is that Cherry organized her collections by themes, and other books touched on other subjects: her interest in science, community, nature, motherhood. All concepts she only touches on in this collection. This is an exciting possibility. Unfortunately, if anything is out there, it's not with us. Experts disagree on dating methods—more will be revealed on the matter in time. However, my instincts point to these poems being relatively modern, even on "ancient" materials. —L. Lincoln]

Stanzas

I watched him through the shimmer [illegible]

Watering his horse in the spring [illegible]
Reached out a hand, never too close to the [illegible]
He might have disappeared forever except for that

Mountain spring that feeds us season after season
That reason for settling, our source of life
Tati whispered one day, her mouth making almost no sound
Cherry you've been a woman forever now, since

We boarded that ship
Her words echoed in my ears like a prayer
How could I have known what was to come
That my mother was right all along

That love brings bondage
That men will leave
Unless they are Desperate men
That a forever girl cannot

Love a minute man

[General consensus among Committee 1 (Lincoln, Bower, Sheldon): this
poem is our most contextual. The only poem where we get a name for our
speaker: Cherry. We strongly believe the term "minute man" refers to a Revolutionary War soldier, potentially the father of her child (referenced in further Stanzas). It's possible that Cherry learned of that term during the war
(first used in 1774) or perhaps after the war, with greater understanding and
reflection on its outcome. Certainly, this poem was written as reflection,
perhaps even decades or generations later, as it seems any relationship had
run its course by drafting. This was our most exciting discovery. We have
sent language and information on physical specimens to early American
historians and linguists. We believe there is potential to name certain sol-
diers serving in that remote area, potentially even find a soldier with a wife
or mistress as Cherry? We can only hope. —B. Sheldon]

The Academia of Desperate

Collected by Kayla Rutledge, Archival Team Member

Welcome to Room #6 on our tour through the Lost Colony of Desperate. Here you will find first hand accounts of academic life in the colony. Archival staff member Kayla Rutledge has unearthed many never before seen records, which have been instrumental in our understanding of Desperate scholarship and the colony's attitude towards Desperate children. Before moving on to the original found documents, we recommend taking time to read Dr. Rutledge's abstract, which summarizes the terminology used when discussing the Colony.

As you exit the room, you may also want to stop into the replica of a Desperate classroom. Choose a desk and use your glasses to join a virtual reality recreation of a class session in progress. You will find age formula practice sheets available in the desks to practice with as you follow along with the lesson. Do you think you would be a good Desperate student?

---

from: krutledge@uncw.edu
to: editors@journal.ET.immortal.org
subject: NEW DISCOVERY + (TO BE PUBLISHED W/ SCHOLAR'S
NOTATIONS)
sent: 09:32am, September 29, 2023

SUBMISSION: Potential Implications of "The Lane Papers" on Social Tensions within the After-Attack Era Colony of Desperate
AUTHOR(S): Dr. Kayla Rutledge (c/o Dr. Kerry Gonzalez)
JOURNAL: "Journal of Extraterrestrial and Immortal Studies, Vol. 1, Issue 3"

Dear editors,

Congratulations on the new journal. The first two issues were spectacular. It's hard to believe that the remains of Desperate were found only three years ago — so much has changed since then. As I'm sure you've heard, my colleague at the University of North Carolina at Chapel Hill, Dr. Kerry Gonzalez, recently uncovered a previously unfound group of documents (hereafter referred to as "The Lane Papers") at the Desperate site back in May. She then approached me to add notations and situate the finding within the larger realm of scholarship. We are now ready to publish our work.

The following papers, worksheets, and grades were recovered in a yellow folder from the remains of one of the structures of Desperate. Writing on the outside of the folder indicates it belonged to Gertie Lane (presumed sister of Essi Lane, town physician from March of the second '18 — unknown).

My article will attempt to accomplish the following:

*1) Draw conclusions about rising social tensions in A.A. (After-Attack)
Desperate that may offer insight into its eventual demise.*

Until recently, the most complete records of Desperate were thought to be the Alami Letters (Rudemiller 2020) and the Physician's Log (Brooks-Flemister 2020) recovered shortly after the explosion. These are what Desperation scholars refer to as P.A. (Pre-Attack) documents. Though scholars disagree on the exact year of the Attack (some documents place it in between the first '35 and the first '50, others in November of the first '63), it is clear that the colony went into hiding at some point during its first century. Little remained to indicate to scholars what may have caused the explosion in the Dioynysian year 2020 (year in Desperation dating unknown).

2) Further Herzog's "Theory of Emotion" by suggesting that Desperate did NOT copy modern printing technology (as assumed by Medina's "Venture Theory"), but instead invented its own within a traditional school setting.

Much confusion has been sparked by A.A. (After Attack) documents and photographs, which seem to indicate that Desperate invented its own technologies (of construction, printing, etc.). Dr. Richard Medina (UC-Berkeley), one of the leading scholars on the colony of Desperate, recently published an article suggesting the residents of Desperate may have ventured outside the colony to "copy" modern-day printing and photography technology. While the colonist's unique dating system has made it impossible to pinpoint Desperate's events on the Dionysian Calendar, it is generally agreed upon that the Attack happened somewhere in the late 1600's (solely because this period is when witch burnings were most popular in North American colonies). Until recently, Medina's "Venture Theory" was the only explanation for printed documents found in the ruins of Desperate. However, recent examination of documents and photographs from Desperate, sparked by renewed interest in Axel Herzog's article in "American Cinematographer", suggests that Desperate settlers invented their own technology.

Until now, there was no telling who or what systems could have invented this technology. The Lane Papers are the first indication Desperate scholars have that the settlement had some sort of school or instructional program.

In conclusion, while many details about Desperate remain unclear, the following documents (along with my notes) provide new insight about the terminology, technology, and social structure of Desperate, as well as some of the rising tensions in the town. Footnotes and interpretations are made by me, Dr. Kayla Rutledge.

Sincerely,

Dr. Kayla Rutledge

—

PROFESSOR, ELLIOTT E. BICYCLE DISTINGUISHED CHAIR,
DEPARTMENT OF EXTERRESTRIAL AND IMMORTAL STUDIES
(CONCENTRATION: AMERICAN SOUTH)
UNIVERSITY OF NORTH CAROLINA WILMINGTON

All mail correspondence to and from the UNC University System is subject to the North Carolina Public Records Law, which may result in monitoring and disclosure to third parties, including law enforcement.

Document 1.1

Name: Gertie Lane   **Age:** 8+D[1]

Fill in the following study guide. Classwide quiz will be on October 23 of the third '49.

- **The Attack:** The mass murder of Original Desperates and Mortal Desperates by outsiders, our reason for sealing off from society,

---

[1]   Instead of grades, delineation appears to occur by Age, an interesting choice considering that almost all Desperate residents After Attack (except for those being born) would have been immortal. Gertie's delineation here indicates that as a physical eight-year-old, she was required to attend school (though by the dating metrics laid out here, if she was 8 at the first '20, she would have been 237 (or 8+D) in the third '49.

resulted in 100 Revisions and 6 deaths (William Alami, Rebecca Alami nee Valencia, etc.)

- **Revision:** When an Original Desperate "dies" and then revives as if nothing has happened. Pending further study, seems harmless.
- **Age Formula** = "Physical age at the time of Desperate founding" (July of the first '20)[2] + "D" (to indicate years Desperate has existed
  - ▫ Mortal Desperate's formula MUST leave off the + D to be correct

$$(S\Rrightarrow)\hbar XV / \twoheadrightarrow 9\aleph = \text{ᕙ}^5\text{α}^6\text{α}\Box(o\nu\text{m})^5 / \text{♩}^3$$

Aging Practice[4]

1. Fred was born in the second '85. How old is he now?
   a. Since Fred was born after the founding of Desperate, he should be measured in Age WITH NO +D. He is 64.
2. Susie was 26 when Desperate was founded. How old is she now?
   a. Since Susie is an Original Desperate, her age is 26+D.
3. Who is older, Susie or Fred?
   a. Fred is older. He is 64. Susie is only 26+D.[5]

---

2   The first recorded firm Desperation dating of the town's founding! This dating is consistent with the Alami Letters, where founding is indicated to have happened before the first '25 (Rudemiller 2020).

3   After careful examination, this mathematical formula is NOT a part of the original printed study guide. This indicates that Lane was doodling this formula (or perhaps inventing it?) while she sat in class taking notes. The formula uses a branch of mathematics unfamiliar to major scholarship. It is a potential invention of some sort of technology unknown to us. The hurried drop off of the square character at the end of the formula indicates Lane was probably reprimanded for her inattention and had to return hurriedly to classwork.

4   Again, this indicates that age was an important social delineation in the Desperate colony.

5   So the physical age of Desperate residents was valued more highly than mental age. The fact that this is a quiz study guide indicates that this idea was codified social strata within the colony. (Though it would have been taught to only mortal children and Original Desperates who were physically school age).

Document 2.1

Scrap paper and two different handwriting indicates these were handwritten notes passed back and forth, probably during school. For clarity, Gertie's writing is in bold. The identity of her unnamed friend is unknown.

> **Are you coming over after school?**
> Can't. Wilhelmina Trout in labor. Have to go help mom deliver the baby.
> **Another Mortal Desperate??**
> We're going to be in school till we're 1,000[6] :(:(:(:(
> **Don't you mean D+9? Don't let him see this[7]**
> Who cares?? I've already learned "The Cherry Poems"[8] about eighty times.
> **Dare you to Revise yourself[9]**
> I'd only miss 10 minutes at most. Plus it might cut into lunch
> **You're right. Un-dare**
> Did you bring your new work for lunch[10]
> **Of course. I made a breakthrough yesterday**
> Oliver will be thrilled
> **What about your designs?**
> Too long to explain here
> **Ok. Meet by the pine tree at lunch**
> We need to go separately to avoid suspicion
> **It's fine. Mortal Desperates don't care at all[11]**
> Oliver cares[12]

---

6   This might mean that physically school-aged Original Desperates were required to attend school as long as there were Mortal Desperates within the colony who were also school-aged.

7   "Him" here probably refers to the instructor. The unnamed friend is physically nine years old.

8   Desperation text, assumed written around the second '50. This book of poems about a young girl who falls in love with someone outside the colony would most likely have been taught as a sort of parable or warning.

9   Probably the verb form of "Revision", indicating she should die to be excused from class activities.

10   It's unclear what this is referring to — it seems that the two were meeting with others (including "Oliver") during lunch, working on individual projects that were far more exciting to them than school.

11   Whatever group the two children are referring to meeting during lunch, it seems to be composed of only Original Desperates.

12   From this, Oliver seems to be indicated as the leader of the secret lunch-time group. The exchange was either cut off or the rest of it has been lost.

Document 3.1

*This document was found torn into pieces within the folder. There is no signa-
ture, indicating that Gertie never gave the document to her parents.*

Dear Parents,

It has come to the school's attention that certain children have been par-
ticipating in an ILLEGAL group during lunchtime. This illegal group, led
by NOTED LAWLESS TROUBLEMAKER AND GENERAL TOWN
OUTCAST Oliver Macabre (Age: 24+D)[13] is completely against the rules of
The Desperate School. Any children found to be participating in this group
WILL BE SENTENCED TO SCHOOL UNTIL THE NINTH '49.

As a reminder, physical age IS THE PRIMARY MARKER OF MAT-
URATION WITHIN DESPERATE. Original Desperates who are physically school-aged MUST attend school, even if they do not enjoy it. It is
very common for children not to enjoy school. All our research shows that
Original Desperates DO NOT progress beyond the capabilities of their
physical age. While we understand that Original Desperates may feel bored,
we are certain that physical-age-appropriate[14] curriculum is the only type of
task they are fit to perform within a society.

One of our common texts, "The Cherry Poems", shows just how tragic it
can be when an Original Desperate begins to think they are older than their
physical age. This is an ILLNESS in children, and will NOT BE TOLER-
ATED. Please see the attached pamphlet for information on how to talk to
your child about the importance of age in society.[15]

Please sign and return this letter to indicate you have read and understand the policy of The Desperate School.

Barry Gillyweed
Head of School

---

13   This is almost certainly the Oliver referenced in Gertie's notes. No documents yet found indicate why Oliver was given the reputation of "Noted Lawless
Troublemaker and General Town Outcast" as attributed to him here. His age, written with the "+D" notation, would mark him as an immortal Original Desperate.

14   That is, curriculum appropriate to one's physical age.

15   The pamphlet has, unfortunately, been lost, or Gertie threw it away.

Document 4.1

Report card for Gertie Lane.

Student: Gertie Lane
Age: 8+D

History: C-

> *Comments*: Gertie frequently refuses to answer test questions according to the textbook ("The Complete History of Desperate: How Self-Immolation Helped Me Discover a Burning Passion for The Story of a Town and a People" by Isaiah Patters). She claims that "Isaiah Patters is not as smart as her", even though he is 17+D and she is only 8+D. Her arrogance makes her a constant frustration in the classroom.

Literature: D+

> *Comments:* Gertie frequently misinterprets "The Cherry Poems" as a feminist text. She seems to willfully miss the point of the story's tragedy. She also turned in the same final essay this year that she turned in five years ago, thinking I wouldn't notice.

Agriculture: B+

> *Comments:* Gertie insists on interrupting nearly every class period and positing new theories of agriculture. This behavior is unacceptable for a child of her age. She does, however, show a real talent for growing tomatoes.

Math: F

> *Comments:* Gertie refuses to understand the Desperation system of aging, even though I have taught it to her nearly one hundred

times. She only began writing the "+D" delineation of her age THIS YEAR!! We do not have high hopes for her going forward as she repeats the year.[16]

Parent's Signature _____

---

16   All indicators within The Lane Papers point to rising tensions in the town of Desperate sometime after the Attack, namely over the strict social structure predicated on physical age. While I am not a psychologist, a strict social order may have been instituted to help Original Desperates more easily ignore their immortality, a condition that the Alami Letters (Rudemiller 2020) and the Physician's Log (Brooks-Flemister 2020) indicate was psychologically painful, especially as the residents began to produce mortal children. This strict social structure also seems to have sparked a secret resistance by some of the Original Desperates — a resistance that may have been working on advanced technology. Whether the rising tensions over age somehow led to the explosion observed in 2020, I leave up to future scholarship and the hopeful discovery of more evidence from the colony.

The Lawson Files
Collected by Archival Team Member, Ali Saleh

Welcome to Room #7 on our tour through the Lost Colony of Desperate. For your penultimate stop, we wanted to take you back to the beginning, just after Desperate was revealed to the world, to the investigation now known as the infamous Lawson files.

These recordings were first found by the Burke County Sheriff's Department on the damaged phone of Richard Lawson. Lawson was hired to tail the newly appointed NC State associate professor, Oliver Macabre. On his final reconnaissance mission, Lawson comes close to the truth of Oliver Macabre before he falls victim to the Attack.

Take a look into the salvaged Lawson files to learn the truth about Oliver and his role in the event that left Desperate permanently destroyed.

We'd like to extend a special thanks to the voice actors at the Royal Company who've generously helped in the recreation of dramatic reenactments, which can be played by flipping down the ear-piece of your glasses and pressing the button when you see an audio icon. There is also blank space in your guide for you to take notes as you listen to the transcript and view pieces of recovered evidence—including Lawson's phone. Do you think you can solve the mystery Lawson was so close to solving?

Remember to go in order and good luck!

Burke County Sheriff's Office—Criminal Investigations Division

Case No: D203X9   **City of** Connelly Springs
Date: August 7, 2020   **County of** Burke
Reporting Officer: Denice Sherrington

Report Summary:
The below recordings were retrieved from the body of Richard Lawson, from the Lawson and Sons Private Investigators. The phone recordings, along with Lawson, were found just outside the explosion site on the night of the mysterious blast. This report has documented all relevant recordings in connection to the ongoing investigation of the explosion and those involved. FBI request for access pending.

Voice Recording Transcription from Richard Lawson

Recording 1.
July 6, 2020 6:38:54 AM.amr

First recording on a new case for a... a uh, Oliver Macabre, male, 24 years old. Teaches at NC State in the agriculture and—what the hell does that say? God damn professors can't write legibly for—In the biological and agricultural engineering department. I need a cigarette. History on Macabre... born and raised in Hickory, North Carolina, received his undergraduate degree and PhD simultaneously from Ghent University in Germany. Received more than just outstanding marks... International Merit Award, Alfred Noble Prize, yadda yadda yadda. Macabre hasn't left his house yet. We're gonna hold tight til he does.

Recording 2.
July 6, 2020 7:14:23 AM.amr

Macabre, after stopping at the Krispy Kreme, wouldn't mind a donut myself, is settling in at his office. With the help of Professor Bowin, we got faculty parking, a front row view through his windows, eyes on his car. Let me see, where did I put that notepad—

Recording 3.

July 6, 2020 3:32:02 PM.amr

Macabre hasn't moved from his office chair. Legs are starting to cramp. The only unusual thing I see around here is the lack of students. Chinese broad at the Shanghai Express across the street nearly called the police 'cause I didn't bring my mask—coronavirus my ass. I don't know—now I don't know one person that's been contracted with Covid-19. How can that be? People telling me it's spreading faster than a god damn wildfire... you know what's real? You know what spreads fast? HPV. That's a real virus, and that shit spreads. That's what they should be educating these kids on. To hell with it.

Recording 4.

July 7, 2020 5:49:58 PM.amr

Trailing Macabre from State. He's turning into the Food Lion... did a follow up while waiting on some of his history, and the old professor's right. Not a whole lot to gather from family or relatives. Not much on social media other than his name next to some awards, buried in a page on Ghent's university web—♫I don't want—who the hell—♫anybody else, when I think about you I touch—Dick speaking. Who? Ronny Smith? HAHAHA you old bastard, how are you? Ahh, I'm working. New case. Uh-huh. Nope, no one's cheating, not that kind of tail. Some, uhh, some fucking little prick over at State. Yeah he's a recent hire, came in guns blazing and pissed off a few people. Mike Bowin. Yeah me neither, til he gave me a call... and he says he wants me to find out what this guy's deal is. Says something ain't right about him. Not natural for someone his age to have contributed this much to the field. Says the kind of research this kid is outputting would have taken decades blah blah blah. Who knows what he's expecting. Of course he's jealous. You know how these academic types are... but I'll tell you what, I might just have to throw some dirt this kid's way if I don't find nothing. Hey pal, that's why they pay me the big bucks... because I can find shit where there ain't none to sniff out. Well, with everyone inside and this bullshit pandemic ruining the country, I don't have a lot of other options—what do you mean it's not bullshit? Oh, shove it up your ass will yah? HA-HAHA you've always been a cock-sucker. Alright, listen, will you fuck off already and let me get back to work? More work than you've ever done HAHAHA alright, say hi to Leanne for me. Alright. Bye. Bye. Fuckin' thing—

Recording 5.

July 14, 2020 6:34:35 PM.amr

Week two on Macabre. Got very little in the way of his daily schedule. Looked into his research a bit. He's in the process of revolutionizing the fertilizer industry. Found a way to concentrate a, uh... to, I guess to distill this fertilizer... da da da...ammonium nitrate...da da da... thousandth degree of current concentration... whatever the hell all that means. Whatever he's doing, he's apparently going to save the industry millions on production costs, transportation, soil regeneration. This guy's shit looks like gold next to everyone else in the department.

Recording 6.

July 17, 2020 11:45:17 PM.amr

Parked on Hillsborough outside Patterson Hall, waiting for our janitor friend to come back with the goods. Shouldn't be more than a few minutes.

Recording 7.

July 18, 2020 12:35:29 AM.amr

Took the bastard long enough... let's see what we got here. Articles. Letters from the department. Insurance... really? What kind of a genius doesn't know the difference between a trash can and recycle bin? What the fuck is this... a middle school play? Desperate Measures: A Play With Music. Didn't think Macabre had any kids...maybe I could get him in as some kind of kiddy freak. Bet old Bowin would love that. And he probably is into that shit, him and the rest of the God damn Democrats. Let's see here... some bills... Security Self-Storage... 3268 Tyron Rd. Could be interesting. We'll hold onto that... oh fuck me, another banana peel?

Recording 8.

August 4, 2020 1:09:10 PM.amr

Bowin got me on the weekend shift. Says Macabre has been making uncharacteristic visits to the office late at night... possibly taking trips out of Raleigh.

Recording 9.

August 4, 2020 1:34:28 PM.amr

Macabre, on Avent Ferry, just turned south down Gorman. Might be headed to that self-storage lot.

Recording 10.

August 4, 2020 2:12:08 PM.amr

Macabre just got back into his car after loading up on some boxes from his storage unit. Not sure what he's up to, but we're gonna keep eyes on him.

Recording 11.

August 4, 2020 2:39:43 PM.amr

Thought Macabre might be stopping at Chapel Hill to break some bread with the hippies, but nope, he's still going. Might have to call Bowin, see if he wants me on him. Might be a good run here.

Recording 12.
August 4, 2020 3:01:25 PM.amr

Just got off the phone with Bowin. Says he wants me on him til the ends of the earth. Wish I'd stopped at the CookOut before heading out... feeling a sweet tea. At least I got Bowin on double-pay for this trip Ha.

Recording 13.
August 4, 2020 4:15:04 PM.amr

He just stopped for gas and thank Mary's sweet ass. Nearly shit my pants HAHA.

Recording 14.
August 4, 4:57:38 PM.amr

Thought Macabre was taking a stop at his hometown in Hickory, but he kept on going til he reached Connelly Springs. Stopped at a... uh, JD's Smokehouse. Could rip into some brisket right now. Might need to stay the night if Bowin is willing to pay for it. Hoping it won't lead to that though 'cause this place fucking sucks.

Recording 15.
August 4, 5:34:58 PM.amr

Here we go. Macabre just pulled off the road about a half mile from JD's like he was going to take a piss. Came back to his car and he's pulling one of the boxes out of his trunk. I'm up ahead on the turn, but I'm gonna try to cut through the brush here and see if I can get some eyes on him.

Recording 16.
August 4, 5:55:11 PM.amr

Got Macabre headed upstream into the wood. Can't see shit. God damn rocks. Just following his light now... Gonna see where he takes us.

Recording 17.
August 4, 6:19:29 PM.amr

Christ, I lost him. Came up to a turn with a wall of trees, paths going every which direction. Lost his light somewhere in the thick back there. Possibly took a left instead of a right, going to backtrack—fucking spider web—going to backtrack and see if I can sniff him out.

Recording 18.
August 4, 6:40:15 PM.amr

I don't know where the fuck he went... took a left, right, around the rock... or was it the other rock? Where am I?

Recording 19.
August 4, 7:02:34 PM.amr

I gone and done it. Lost him.   forest soiree. I didn't sign up for a
Now... back at the creek, or at least   fuckin—
I think I'm back at the creek, road
should be up ahead. Bowin better bring it up to triple pay for this

Final Notes:
Lawson's phone was recovered with minimal damage. His recordings con-
firmed that Macabre was storing large amounts of amonomium in his storage unit on Gorman street. A new investigation will now open into Lawson's
connections with the blast as well as his PI methods for unlawful practice
and general fuckery.

The Professor's Dilemma
Collected by Michael Ivory, Archival Team Member

Welcome to Room #8 on our tour through the Lost Colony of Desperate. What follows begins with an email that our archival staff member sent in the year 2024 to his colleague at the University of Miami, about four years after the reveal of Desperate.

The "attachment" is a series of diary entries from Gertie Lane, a long-standing Desperate citizen. Gertie mentions "craving mortals" in these entries with a specificity that suggests, as the 'Cherry Poems' did, that the citizens of Desperate—at times—had contact with the outside world; although direct evidence of this, to date, has not been found. Some residents of Connelly Springs, recalling unknown gaps in their family trees or a family history of lengthy longevity, claim to be descendants of Desperate, although all have rejected requests to submit DNA tests at this time.

If you would rather listen to the entries, you may use the earpiece paired with your glasses for a dramatic reading from child actress and Daytime Emmy winner Plum Kravitz-Blum. We do suggest, however, looking at the documents as you do so—as seeing the original diary pages, in Gertie's scrawling hand, is a rare opportunity.

from: m.j.ivory@umiami.edu
to: jolivarez@umiami.edu
subject: HIGH IMPORTANCE – Desperate discoveries
sent: 02:25 am, March 15, 2024

Body:

Juan,

I know this is an odd time for emails but you also know my circadian rhythm has two left feet. Anyways, attached may be the most significant discovery to date concerning the history of Desperate, and how a community of functionally immortal people could cease to exist. The following is a set of transcriptions of recovered journal entries by one Gertie Lane (See Rutledge in Vol 1. Issue 3. of JEIS), the existence of which I am almost certain was only known to her. There are also scans of some interesting scribbles that give us a glimpse into her hyperactive mind. To say that Gertie was smart is an understatement. I found myself rather frightened on occasion reading her thoughts. And yet, I can't help but note how "justified" this felt. This has certainly kept me up at night, to say the least. Anyway, please let me know what you think ASAP. I'm pretty sure something like this could do wonders for our case for a "Mortality Studies" department, or at least a specialized division in the Anthropology department.

Best,

Michael Ivory, Jr.
—

ASSOCIATE PROFESSOR OF ANTHROPOLOGY
UNIVERSITY OF MIAMI
PHONE: (***) ***-**** | MI.J.IVORY@UMIAMI.EDU

Jan 18 '20

Foreseer Jakes (that pile of pig slop) just hates me. I try to tell Mom that he doesn't understand teaching.[17] He only understands telling people what to do. And that I'm just as Original as he is! I remember just as much as he does! And the whole "+D" thing doesn't matter! It's not like they see me as a "+D" anyway. If they did, I wouldn't be going to this stupid school! I could be helping us figure out how to live a life worth living.

Oliver says that death is a gift, because it "makes the hands work faster and makes the heart seek a truth." Of course, truth is subjective. That means it changes for everybody. If I swam to the middle of the ocean, my arms would give out and I would drown and Revise until I could get to shore. But whales probably see all the blue water and feel free. Like that, subjective. But those are still our truths. And dying makes you crave that truth. At least that's what Oliver says.

Still, I think I agree. It's why I crave mortals. As friends. As lovers. Even as enemies. I crave them, because their urgency drives me. Everything could be "the last time" so they make it count. They like pretty things because they think they might not ever get a chance to see a pretty thing again. I just drink the daffodils and pine trees like water. They savor it like wine. I like that. But Foreseer Jakes wants me to cling to a "+D" like that's all I could ever be. NO.

I'm meeting with Oliver and the others this evening. I'm excited. Maybe there are a few of us who care.

Until. [18]

March 7, '20

Today I watched a cut bleed. It hurt, but I didn't go ask for help. Not just because I knew it would fix itself, though. I just watched how some of the blood dripped from me and onto the floor of the bathroom at school. And

---

17   "Foreseer" seems to be a term analogous to "Teacher". I'm not sure what is so particular about instructors that they would garner such a title. What do they see ahead of or to?

18   An interesting closing. I find that in general, time-based greetings are left off, unless absolutely necessary for information passage. In some funny way, "Until" seems to be Gertie's (or a general Desperate) way of saying that there is no need to name a time. The time will always be there. Perhaps I'm waxing a bit too poetic. I shouldn't speak so definitively on such an obscure culture.

when the cut disappeared, my blood was still there, on the floor.

Some of me did not just go away. Some of my fibers remained separate.[19] Almost...free? Regeneration is a funny thing.

I'll talk to Oliver about it a little bit later.

Until.

Mar 8 '20

Oliver loves my idea. It makes sense: if we can't die because we regenerate, then all we have to do is figure out how to separate our bodies past the point of regeneration. At the very least, even if our fibers persist in living, they won't be able to reform organs if they are far enough apart. We need something big to sever our bodies beyond repair. I don't know if we will truly "die" if our fibers remain intact. But maybe, without brains, we won't have consciousness. And maybe that limbo will be a reprieve?

Oliver says that even if the plan doesn't work the way we want, at the very least Desperate won't be able to hide anymore. Maybe we'll be able to Venture, if we still live past this.

Until.

Mar 29 '20

The tomatoes worked. They're letting me run a new project. Foreseer Pryce has always been nice to me, which makes me want to learn in her class. It's why I have a B+ I guess. She says I'm "precocious." Of course I am. I'm not just smart for my age, I am always older than my age. Isn't that what "+D" means?

Anyway, they won't suspect me asking for the fertilizer for my project. I feel bad lying to Foreseer Pryce. But I also know that we've been shut out from our truths. Maybe we can all find it this way.

Until.

---

19   Separation from contemporary learning, and the lack of urgency to learn how to mend bodies that are perpetually perfect, has led to some divergence from typically endorsed theory on human biology. "Fibers" here appears to be the Desperate answer to "cells" in our world. It is not clear if this is because Desperate bodies are indeed structured differently at the sub-tissue level, or if the people of Desperate were spitballing theory.

[Below image: Formulas? I emailed Kayla over at UNC Wilmington to see if she knew anything about these formulas. Seems the math department there is stumped. But I believe she was testing some parameter of the limits of "Revision". Why was she apologizing to Oliver, though?]

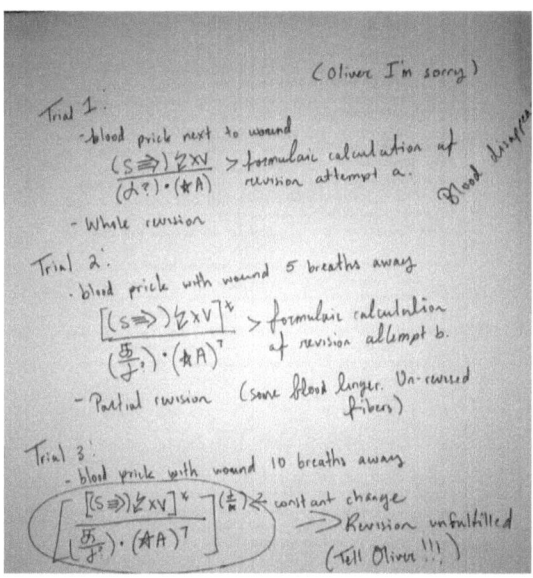

May 10 '20

We're coming up on the school play. I hate that lie we tell ourselves every year. Just like that foolish mess Isaiah Patters wrote. The best thing Isaiah could have done after burning himself alive was staying burnt. Quietly.

There's a part in the play that I just cannot stand because it's just not true to what happened. You would think that a historical play written for a town of people who were all there for its real-life inspiration would want to keep its facts straight. But of course, it's written by a Gillyweed, so everyone goes with it and I end up with a C- in history. How uninspired.

The Gillyweeds get away with everything. Every year they do this cursed excursions and they always choose Isaiah Patters or that unbearable Anna Gillyweed, just because they are older and more respected than us younger students. They have seen the world and they wear that sight like a crown none of us will ever get to inherit. Even when we cannot die, we make life frightening and painful.

Anyway, Oliver says since that part is the crowd-favorite part of the play,

I can use that spot to make our declaration. I would like nothing better.

Until.

July 9 '20

Oliver told us he has to disappear for a while. He says we are on the verge of freedom and that he has found someone who can help us. But he says he's being followed, and he doesn't want to risk the plan or our safety before it is time. I hope he will be alright.

Until.

July 16 '20

Headmaster asked me if I knew anything about the "Let Cherry Speak" flyers around school. Of course, I said no. I don't know if he believed me. If anybody has spoken up for Cherry, I have. Cherry tried to tell us she was suffering, just like most of us are now. We just don't admit it!

Just the other day, I overheard this girl crying in the bathroom because she was afraid to love anyone. She said if she loved, then she might have a child. And if she had a child, that child would die. This is how they keep us from Venturing![20] From feeling!

I don't deny it might hurt to outlive your children. But keeping us frozen in life by making us attend school forever to "protect us" is prison! And I am not a prisoner!

Cherry and Desperate will have their day.

Until.

P.S. I haven't heard from Oliver yet and it's making me worry. The others are telling me just to focus on maintaining the fertilizer reserves. That Oliver will be back and that I should just focus on being ready.

July 20 '20

Oliver came back, and he brought a man with him. The man dresses stranger than any man I have seen in Desperate. His hair is longer than any of the women, and he pulls it back into a long ponytail. His name is Profes-

---

20   "Venturing" in this context means not only to physically wander, but also to allow one's mind to wander. It is a rather political sentiment, taken up by Gertie, Oliver, and many of the others.

sor Gil James and he works in agriculture at the local university.[21]

The Professor and Oliver love each other. I can tell, even though Oliver tries to be coy in front of us. (I wonder if he still thinks of me as a child whose innocence he has to protect?)

Here in Desperate, most love is between men and women, because we focus so much on what can replace the mortal children we lose with time. To see Oliver and Gil loving each other is...different. But I don't hate it. In fact, I see that there is so much more to life than what Desperate is offering us. I'm happy Oliver got to have that.

Gil taught us about the fertilizer, and how different substances can do different things depending on how you use them. I already knew ammonium nitrate was combustible, but this stuff is powerful! He says that in a place called Bay-root, a lot of people got hurt because of it. I don't think he knew we were intending to use the fertilizer for that. Oliver just kept asking questions, and Gil answered with smiles because he thought we were just fascinated with fire. Does Gil even know we are immortal?

It made me nervous. Hearing how much pain it caused to so many mortal people made me wonder if we were doing the right thing. I don't want people to hurt just because. But then I remember us crying in bathroom stalls and never growing up in our bodies or in their eyes.

Gil seems so alive in his love for Oliver. Oliver smiles back at him, but it doesn't sound the same. To be fair, I don't even understand Gil's excitement. And I realize that there's a hollowness in me. I think it's in all of us who cannot die. Maybe we're all just like the dead trees. Still standing, but rotten.

Until.

July 17 '20

I have been avoiding writing because as we get closer, I want to think about it less and less. But I know it's the right thing. Still, Foreseer Pryce smiled at me today and it made me feel good just a little bit. It made me think of what I was sacrificing.

And it made me pause and think that maybe we could redeem Desperate. But I know better.

Until.

---

21   North Carolina State University

[Below image: Appears to be a set of notes consistent with lessons perhaps offered by one Professor Gil James before his resignation following Desperate's demise.]

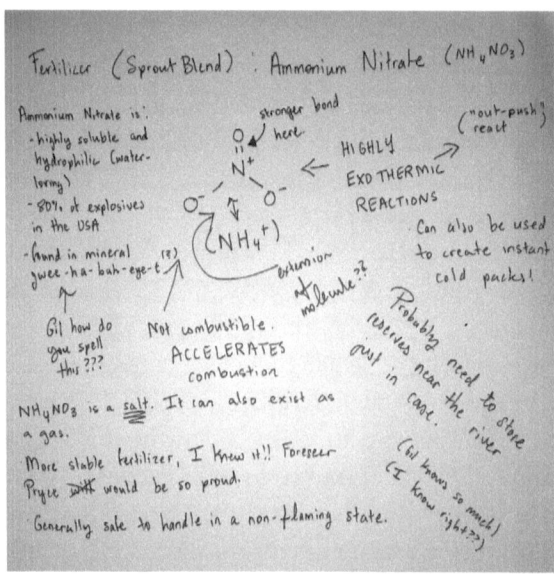

July 29 '20

Everything I did was in the name of freedom. All of life has been a cage. My body is a cage that refuses to release me. This town is a cage that wants to choke me into submission.

I did not mean for my writing to be discovered. I just wanted to know what life was like outside of this bondage. But I saw how they received Cherry, and it doesn't matter that they do not know that they are rejecting me. They have shown their faces, so we will show our hand.

Soon, we will make our bid for justice.

Until,

Cherry[22]

---

22   It seems that "Cherry" never lived but was instead a figure invented by Gertie in a bid to incite thought among Desperations. It must have been so frustrating to see her work morphed into a tool of social control. It's funny how Desperate is the name of the town, and the perfect word to describe this last "bid for justice." Two opposing groups with the same name.

Desperate Measures

Collected by Catey Christiansen, Archival Team Member

Welcome to Room #9 on our tour through the Lost Colony of Desperate. Please take your seats. LIVE full-cast re-enactments of the play "Desperate Measures" occur each Saturday and Sunday at 11AM, 1PM, and 3PM. If you've come on a weekday, or can't wait until one of the scheduled showings, you may also use your glasses to view the virtual reality version, though we highly recommend the live version if possible.

This play, once thought to be strange and insignificant (as noted in an e-mail exchange at the entrance of the exhibit), has since become a cornerstone in the discovery and understanding of Desperate. It has become absolutely revelatory in the parsing of what exactly led to the reveal of Desperate, NC and who were the major players involved. Feel free to sit back, relax and follow along with the script provided in your Field Guide.

Note: Our archivist for Room #9 has also broken down the significance of each section of the play to further your understanding, which is included in the back of this section for your convenience.

from: clchrist@uncg.edu
to: mi.j.ivory@umiami.edu
subject: Desperate Measures
sent: 01:29 pm, March 28, 2024

Body:

Michael,

Here is the script you requested from our archives. Still not sure why we hold onto it. We have tried to analyze it and even had undergrads who talked about producing it, but I convinced them that it was drivel. Can you clue me in on why this holds significance?

Regards,

Catey Christiansen
—
ASSOCIATE PROFESSOR OF THEATRE
UNIVERSITY OF NORTH CAROLINA AT GREENSBORO
PHONE: (***) ***-**** | CLCHRIST@UNCG.EDU

Desperate Measures
A Play with Music
Written by Anna Gillyweed

Cast List	
Anselm Ansoma	9+D
Petra Ansoma	10
Davey Branscomb	11
Charlie Branscomb	16
Norman Gillyweed	17
Ondine Gillyweed	13
Petunia Gillyweed	9
Quincy Gillyweed	5
Estye Gold	15+D
Ivan Gold	6
Gertie Lane	8+D
Isaiah Patters	17+D
Peter Sambutina	7+D
Naomi Sambutina	14+D
Ginny Trout	11
Geoffrey Trout	13
Viola Valencia	10+D
Olivia Valencia	10+D
Director	
Anna Gillyweed	17+D

Head of School
Barry Gillyweed

Director's Notes

The play is to be performed each year on the Courtyard's OakWillow Stage, built after the minor relocation of our village about 100 years ago when the Outsiders flooded the River to make it a Lake. Parents and other adults gather on the courtyard lawn midday to watch, emblazoned by the sun. Our stage was built around trees - a mighty ancient oak bursts through the upper left corner of the larger left stage (make sure to trim stage-hole to accommodate growth every ten years) and our willow on the smaller right platform is about 20 years old right now. By the time she fills the hole cut into the stage, about 10-20 years from now, she will be at the end of her life, we will cut her down, make beautiful things of her corpse, and plant a new one in her stead.

The setting for each scene is suggested by use of quick-change costume pieces, hand props, rolling furniture pieces, and 3, 3 sided rotating flats (1.Wood walls, 2.Trees, 3.Blue paintings with white fuzzy lines that could be interpreted as sky with wispy clouds or a transparent barrier.)

Special thanks to:
The Gillyweed family
The Ansoma Family
The Trout Family
The Patters
Mr. Ming
Preacher Lawson
Franny Ledbetter
Mr. and Mrs. Alami
Lily Everstone
Foreseer Cooper
Foreseer Jakes
Foreseer Pryce

SCENE I: DESPERATE MEASURES

[*At the start of our scene, the three rotating flats are turned to blue skies. The ensemble enters, with props to make it clear they are on a boat heading across the ocean.*]

ISAIAH At the beginning of time, our brave people transversed the great ocean. It was not an easy passing.

DOCTOR/GEOFFREY [*writing a letter*] A flesh disintegrating red fever has gripped many on this boat. The likes of which were so unusual the devil himself could not have imagined it into creation.

RED SCOURGE OF DEATH/NORMAN [*evil laughter*]

DOCTOR/GEOFFREY I fear not one child will survive this gruesome scourge. At least God granted us the gift of its swiftness, no long suffering hours to tend, just melt and gone.

RED SCOURGE OF DEATH/NORMAN Yummy.

DOCTOR/GEOFFREY Making the sea swell with the tears of our parents, we have tossed thirty unrecognizable bodies overboard. I question the parents who thought wee toddlers and infants could withstand this passage. It is my greatest hope that we still get to welcome Tati Sena's child into the village we will raise when we make land.

ISAIAH The doctor was the last to succumb to the illness. As our people offered their last sacrifice to the sea, they looked out on the horizon for hope.

[*They carry the Doctor's body and dump him over the edge of the stage. Ivan and Ginny are waving blue fab-*

ric in the pit between the audience and the stage. Their ocean swallows the body. They then move onto the stage. As a storm.*]*

ANSELM But instead, a preter-natural tempest was descending upon us.

ESTYE The wind whipped up as soon as the doctor's body was no longer visible in the waves.

GERTIE It was as if a gigantic grey beast lunged for our ship from above.

TEMPEST BEAST/CHARLIE
[*Pours water on them and growls.*]

OLIVIA Walls of water descended upon us. Great claws of waves tossed us like a cougar batting a baby rabbit for hours before a meal.

TEMPEST BEAST/CHARLIE
[*Beats the Passengers side to side. Growls again. The passengers drop to the ground.*]

VIOLA We hid in the lower depths, laying on the floor so as not to get slammed into the hull, so sickened and terrified.

NAOMI (Come up to pray.) Our mourning became praying.

ENSEMBLE We heard voices.

ISAIAH And then just as suddenly, came the dawn. Two days later, stunned and morose, we made land. One hundred forty three boarded, one hundred disem-barked in what is at this present moment called North Carolina. On the shore, our people fell flat, wide armed, embracing the sands and or running to rest their weary bodies against the wild olive trees and wind gnarled oaks. Couples kissed and the last of our children frolicked in the surf. Until:

[*Mosquitoes enter onto Right platform*]

WALTER MOSQUITO/PETUNIA
Hey, Mortimer, look over there. What is that?

MORTIMER MOSQUITO/QUINCY
I don't know Walter, but they sure smell good.

WALTER MOSQUITO/PETUNIA
Let's go check them out!

[*The two mosquitoes flank Isaiah and bite him. Isaiah tries to swat them away. They fly just far enough away that Isaiah can't reach them.*]

MORTIMER/QUINCY Walter, that was Deee-licious.

WALTER/PETUNIA Like nothin' I aint never tasted. (He thinks.) Mortimer, are you thinkin' what I'm thinkin'?

MORTIMER/QUINCY Whatchoo thinkin', Walter? (he realizes what Walter is thinkin')

WALTER/PETUNIA Let's tell everyone we know!

MORTIMER/QUINCY Heya, Millie! Hey Lance! All y'all fellers - come check this out.
[*they hold up a prop representing a swarm of mosquitoes*]

[*The mosquitoes run after the settlers on attack. Isaiah leads the escape, leaping off of the stage and circling the audience followed by the screaming settlers and the swarm of mosquitoes.*]

ISAIAH The swarm was as otherworldly, as thick and impenetrable as the monster storm cloud we had faced out at sea.

[*As Isaiah finally gets enough ahead, the mosquitoes disappear and all the*

settlers sit on the edge of the central stage, Isaiah center.]

ISAIAH We ran for days, along the river, until they finally stopped following us.

[*Panting, exhausted, the ensemble lays on the stage, then arises slowly as if from the dead to sing:*]

Desperate Measures

ENSEMBLE
We follow the river
'Til we are delivered
Through journey as long
As a season we sailed.

The ocean it swallowed
Our hearts as it hollowed
Out parts of our psyches
While everyone ailed

We run through the wringer
Escaping the stinger
Of swarms of mosquitoes
Collapse in this spot

ENSEMBLE
It's desperate measures

TATI [*Coming forward holding her very pregnant belly*]
Let's unload our treasures

The baby is coming
NOW! Like it or not.

ENSEMBLE [*unpacking*]
Desperate Measures
We found here our tethers

LILY [*tending to Tati*]
A fire, heat some water
Some clean linens, dear.

[*A villager nods and goes to get things ready.*]

TATI Oh Mary, my mother,
Please send me another
Please let this one make it
I'm shaking in fear.

[*Musical Interlude. A ballet. Members of the ensemble spread out before the two women and then shroud them in fabric.*]

LILY [*not visible, behind shroud– spoken*] Push. Push. Come on Tati.

[*We hear a scream from Tati, then nothing. Then quiet sobbing. All the while, a ballet downfront representing the loss of life. The ensemble drops the shroud to the floor and part to reveal Lily and Tati grieving.*]

ENSEMBLE
It's desperate measures

Our pain and our pleasures
Root into the earth here
Our lost ones we rue.
We've found a new village
Where we will not pillage
Because it is ours for
the taking. We do.

ISAIAH Welcome to Desperate.
Population 100.

[*Exeunt All.*]

SCENE 2: WE DIE, WE LIVE, AT ONCE

ANSELM We built our homes along the river.

ESTYE Settled in quite nicely. No local tribes seemed to claim this little swath of land.

PETER The Gillyweeds set up a school for our few children, and our farms began to thrive. Families started to grow.

NAOMI But our original children didn't grow. Parents held their children back in school, worried about their development. Maybe the scourge of red fever had stunted their growth.

VIOLA Children born in Desper-

ate started to outgrow those who
had journeyed over the sea.

We Die, We Live, at Once

AGATHA/ONDINE
My death from birth
I'm gauze wrapped and
herbed
Eyes flutter wide
My husband disturbed

SAMBUTINA/DAVEY
Crushed by a tree
Goodbye family.

MRS. SAMBUTINA/PETRA
Heave off that trunk
Oh, Humanity!

ENSEMBLE
We die, we live, at once

ISAIAH
Despite my many stunts.

ENSEMBLE
It frightens and excites.
Surviving blows and blights

VALENCIAS
Skate ice lake crack
Slip and slide under
Eyes frozen wide
Wait, thaw, live wonder

MING/GINNY
Shot in a duel
Gone for a moment
Bodies revise
Not my opponent

ENSEMBLE
We die, we live, at once

MORTAL CAST
Developmental runts

ENSEMBLE
It frightens and excites.
Surviving blows and blights.

OLIVIA Back in those days, before
we knew, and as other villages
developed around us, many Desperates would Venture regularly
to the world outside.

ANSELM We even married outsiders and brought them into our
dear village.

PETER But all of this interaction
meant that Non-Desperates
eventually bore witness.

ESTYE And they did not take
kindly to our gift.

GERTIE Frightened and threaten-
ing, they attacked us screaming
through the night.

NAOMI With their torches, pick-axes, pitchforks, and swords.

[*The adult audience has committed this section to memory and participates in the performance in the role of "The Outsiders", shouting at the actors on stage.*]

Reprise:

OUTSIDERS
> You die. You live.
> Witchcraft you devils!
> Burn and slay all
> Scatter their vessels.

[*The ensemble pantomimes a brutal attack with fabric flames surrounding. They all fall to the ground and then slowly arise save a few parents and partners who come to life, but stay low to mourn the loss of their young and adult children born in Desperate and outsiders who had married in.*]

ENSEMBLE
> We die, we live, at once
> Through illnesses and brunts
> We now know we revise
> Watch out for others' eyes.

[*Exeunt All.*]

SCENE 3: THE BALLAD OF CHERRY

OLIVIA Before the Attack, Desperate teens thought themselves above their station.

VIOLA Before our wise leaders designed aging equations. Before the town council's edict on compulsory schooling of physical minors, wild girls and boys could cast aside their education and run willy nilly.

OLIVIA Chaos ensued.

VIOLA Yearning for intimacy and connection, some young Desperates sought companionship outside of our protective boundaries.

OLIVIA It was thought that our inventions could mask our borders, but it was not until after the attack that our situation necessitated designing the advanced stages of security we have in place nowadays.

VIOLA Several teen girls succumbed to the drive. One such poor soul was our sweet misguided Cherry, who tragically fell for a rebel soldier.

The Ballad of Cherry

[*String trio starts to play. Enter Naomi and Estye, crossing down center. They are both wearing the Cherry costume and alternate playing the part of Cherry as penance for not admitting which one of them wrote the now canonical poems. Rearrangements by Anna Gillyweed.*]

CHERRY 1

On that maiden voyage
I was a maiden still
The gift of blood became me
While my friends, red fever fell

CHERRY 2

For years they all insisted

ENSEMBLE

You're too young to be a bride
Perhaps not yet at fifteen,

CHERRY 2

Perhaps I'm twenty-five

CHERRY 1

Then thirty, forty, who knows

ENSEMBLE

We stopped noticing the seasons

CHERRY 2

Desire scorned and scoffed at

ENSEMBLE

Never giving valid reasons

ENSEMBLE

Cherry you're too bawdy.
Cherry you're so crass.
Cherry you're too tawdry.

CHERRIES

We discover the crack in the glass.

CHERRY 1

How could I have known what was to come

CHERRY 2

That my mother was right all along

CHERRY 1

That love brings bondage.
That men will leave

CHERRY 2

Unless he is a Desperate man

CHERRIES

That a forever girl cannot
Love a minute man

[*The soldier enters. Cherry peeks through the "glass".*]

CHERRY 1

> I watched him through the
> shimmer shadow
> Water his horse in the spring
> by the fissure
> Reached out a hand, never
> close to the shallows
> Step through now and meet
> him, my lover, my gallows

[*The soldier collapses onto the stage
and sees Cherry. Spoken:*]

SOLDIER/NORMAN Oh vision.
From whence did you come?

CHERRY 2 You are injured. Let
me tend your wounds.

ANSELM Cherry cared for the soldier at the village borders.

PETER Built him a tent. Cloaked
him from view.

ANSELM Day after day. Cleaned
him and fed him.

PETER By the time he could walk
again, her underdeveloped body
was already in the throes of
morning sickness.

VIOLA Cherry brought her soldier
home. Overwrought, the council mistakenly decided to allow

Cherry to serve as an apprentice
to the Physician.

OLIVIA She married her man and
birthed her babe.

GERTIE Two years later, he left
without a word.

VIOLA And two years after that,
the attack took their child.

Reprise:

CHERRY 1

> How could I have known
> what was to come

CHERRY 2

> That my mother was so right
> all along

CHERRY 1

> That love brings bondage.
> That men will leave.

CHERRY 2

> Unless he is a Desperate man

CHERRIES

> That a forever girl cannot
> Love a minute man

[*Exeunt All.*]

FINALE: DESPERATE MEASURES

PETRA That was all a long long time ago. Our Ventures take on a different form now.

DAVEY We are safe from the world. Thanks to our brilliant inventions, no one can find Desperate, and no one ever will again.

CHARLIE Sometimes, we students even get to kick in a few contributions to the incredibly innovative research and technological development here in Desperate. Our adult population has been responsible for advancements that far exceed that of the outside world. It is unbelievable what gets unlocked in the fully developed immortal brain.

ISAIAH Our mortal children grow and thrive and assist our research, also sometimes contributing dynamic and beneficial ideas of their own. All here in Desperate, mortal or not, share the drive and desire for discovery and invention within our closed community. All are at peace.

ONDINE After the unanticipated flooding of our dear river by the companies harnessing the power of water, we had to move our entire village even closer to outside populations.

PETUNIA Innovation went over and above what we thought possible, allowing us to move quickly, effectively, and permanently mask our existence from the Outside gaze.

QUINCY But having been caught off guard that one time, we designed a method to prevent future disasters.

IVAN Every ten years since the flood, we embark upon a Venture Summit and Synthesis.

GINNY Desperate Adults volunteer and one student representative is chosen by the Head of School. The committee travels to cultural locations outside of our village to gather current data on world culture.

GERTIE However, most of our discoveries are in-house, sprung from our brilliant leaders' minds.

ENSEMBLE No longer desperate, we Desperates thrive.

Reprise: Desperate Measures

ENSEMBLE

It's desperate measures
Our pain and our pleasures
Root into the earth here
Our lost ones we rue.
We've found a new village
Where we will not pillage
Because it is ours for
the taking. We do.

[*Exeunt All.*]

[*Curtain Call.*]

ALTERNATE FINALE:
DESPERATE MEASURES
by Gertie Lane

[*Secret performance ambush inserted after Scene 3.*]

ANSELM That was all a long long time ago. And it didn't really happen that way, anyway.

PETER We are safe from the world, but prisoners of our own childish bodies.

ESTYE By the way - it was us students who have been responsible for generating most of our village's advancements, with no credit given.

NAOMI It is unbelievable what gets locked up in a child's immortal brain.

VIOLA And we are Desperate. Desperate for release from this infinite drudgery.

OLIVIA But with help from one who escaped, we found a solution.

IMMORTAL ENSEMBLE [*spoken in unison*] No longer desperate, wish Desperates goodbye.

Desperate Measures Reprise:

ENSEMBLE

It's desperate measures
Our pain and our pleasures
Burst out to the ether
With lost ones we rue.
We set loose our village
No longer we pillage
Free children imprisoned
We can and we do.

EPILOGUE

IMMORTAL ENSEMBLE Let Cherry speak. Let Cherry speak. Let Cherry speak. Let Cherry speak. (Gertie comes forward.)

GERTIE I am Cherry. It was me all along. I am sorry, Estye and Naomi. They were just creative musings of my longing for what you had that I could never be in this eight year old body. They were never meant to be used to punish you. I should have said something so, so long ago. I will make it up to you all. I promise.

Cast the First Stone

GERTIE/CHERRY
Cast the first stone if you will.
Before you do, please ask yourself:
How long must a girl stay a child

and never become a woman?

I only watch my own reflection.
Some dark magic
and all these glass walls
keep us hidden from the world.

Always a maiden, never a maid.
I asked him to toss the granite
ever so gently, a simple shattering
Do not fear my soft curls and my bare garden.

[*Cherry tosses the granite.*]

[*Boom. EXEUNT ALL.*]

Archival Notes Breaking Down The Significance of "Desperate Measures"

"Desperate Measures: a play with music" was written by immortal child, Anna Gillyweed, daughter of the school's headmaster. It was performed yearly on the OakWillow Stage by the entire student population for all residents of the town. The immortal children always play the same roles, the aging mortal children get shifted around each year.

Within the text of the play, some of the mythology of Desperate is revealed.

Scene 1: The journey from the old world involved the contraction of a mysterious red fever that killed many of the travelers. A horrible otherworldly storm also ravaged them before they made land in what is now North Carolina. Upon landing, a biblical-scale attack by local mosquitoes chased the remaining travelers far inland to what is now the village of Desperate. The scene ends with the delivery of a baby who does not survive.

Scene 2: They settle in the foothills of the Blue Ridge Mountains and build the town of Desperate along the Catawba River. They start noticing strange things. Children who made the voyage do not grow, but children who are born in Desperate do. Despite mortal wounds, the original settlers seem to come back to life. As settlers would sometimes venture outside of Desperate, or as outsiders married in, suspicion began to mount about these curiosities. A group of non-settlers attacks Desperate, but even though the mob kills them all off, every original settler comes back to life.

Scene 3: A teenaged immortal named Cherry falls in love with a revolutionary officer, a few years before the mob attack. Although the community frowns upon teenagers having relationships, Cherry is impregnated by the soldier and they marry. The soldier leaves Cherry after two years together and then their child is killed in the mob attack. The mortal-born toddler does not revive.

Note: this section is a performative penance. There are two teen-aged immortal girls who got pregnant around the same time. When the Cherry poems were discovered, neither girl would admit to writing them and so in punishment, they both are forced to perform the part of Cherry as a cautionary tale, every year. Both still contend they did not write the poems.

Finale: Advanced technology invented by Desperate adults now protects the community from outsider discovery. Desperates stopped leaving, for the most part, in order to remain insular and safe. The community was caught by surprise in 1925 when Duke Power flooded the Catawba to harness hydropower with the Rhodhiss Dam. They had to move the whole village with very little notice. In order to prevent future disasters, they send representatives out on a Venture Summit to collect outsider information.

Alternate Finale: This copy of the play includes an alternate ending, written by Gertie Lane with the support of most of the immortal students. It reveals that most of the advanced technology was developed by the students, not adults. They are fed up with the non-negotiable hierarchical practices of adult Desperates. In secret meetings with escaped resident and brilliant academic, Oliver Macabre, a majority of the immortal students decide to take action. Based on the research of Gertie Lane, they revise the finale.

Gertie reveals that she was the one who wrote the Cherry poems as a playful imagining of what it would be like to have had slightly more agency trapped in a teenaged body rather than an 8 year old one with no hope for a sexual life. When the poems were discovered and made canon for school instruction, she could not bring herself to admit the poems were hers. She apologizes to Estye and Naomi for causing them to take responsibility and receive punishment. The finale ends with the public destruction of the community through the detonation of a hand-made bomb (referred to as "the granite," a reference to a canonical Cherry poem.) –C

Tree Rings

Collected by Archival Team Member, Paul Watts-Offret

Welcome to Room #10 on our tour through the Lost Colony of Desperate. What follows is a very special addition to the collection.

Tree Rings by C.J. Bradley is a collection of short stories set in the forests of North Carolina during a time of subsistence living long lost in our contemporary age. Each story centers on a different young protagonist, following that young person through innocent childhood games and sometimes disturbing fantasies.

The stories themselves read like innocuous, if somewhat dark, versions of Little House on the Prairie. What caught the attention of Desperate scholars was the titular story of the collection, a brief piece that introduces a mysterious immortal old woman who serves as an omniscient narrator for each story in the collection.

C.J. Bradley took the world by storm after being outed, live, during the now-infamous interview with Stephen Colbert. The mysterious old woman— now thought to be a character based on fact, rather than fiction— has led scholars and internet-sleuths alike to revisit the stories, reading with near surgical precision, looking for Desperate clues. As such, stories have proved to be an invaluable resource in understanding the fateful events that transpired two decades ago.

Find a seat in one of our many cozy armchairs in the reading nook on the far side of the room. A copy of the titular story, "Tree Rings" is reproduced in your printed field guide, so that you can read at your own leisure. If you would prefer the audio version, you can sit back and listen, in the author's own voice, by employing the audio-capability on your glasses when you see the audio icon. A first-edition copy of her collection of stories is also on display under glass, for your viewing. You may also wish to view a clip of C.J.'s revealing interview, which is playing on a loop near the room exit. Please enjoy: "Tree Rings."

Tree Rings

By C.J. Bradley

What does it feel like to be a tree? Trees could be sentient beings for all we know. Trees breathe, just like we do; they even sleep at night and wake in the morning. If you've spent multiple human lifetimes watching them, as I have, then you begin to see their personality. I see their branches and leaves settle in for the night. They droop, just slightly, as night falls, and the trees' internal organs slow down; the pulling of water from the roots up to the leaves reduces to a crawl. When the sun rises, the trees inhale and stretch, expanding their branches and leaves, much like the bronchi in the human lungs that splits like branches to pull oxygen out of the air we breathe. Trees know when other trees around them have been hurt; they react to that pain by protecting themselves, and once a tree is an adult, it's impossible to know just how old it is without cutting it open and looking at the rings.

An old woman is a lot like a tree, and I'm an old woman in more ways than one. No one wants to think about what it's like to be old forever. The young can't see the old, and the old become like the trees, just part of the landscape. But at least youth can't be imposed on me, though what's 80 years to 500? Age in this place is a tragic irony.

It's nobody's fault. We aren't supposed to live forever. Trees may have evolved to live for hundreds and thousands of years (they had a head start), but not humans. The human brain was built for just one lifetime, which makes it selfish. We hardly understand our own mental experience and have no way of understanding the mental experiences of other creatures. Maybe if humans could truly understand what it's like to be a tree... but that's un-likely to happen, even with our technology.

So I sit amongst the oaks, shaded and cool, and I watch. I come and go as I please; nobody notices. I go unnoticed even in the world outside our secluded one hundred. The young expose their secrets to me because I'm too old to be seen. I'm the secret keeper they never knew they had. I know what they are going to do before they do it. I've heard their declarations of love. "I'll never stop loving you." "Your love is all I need for a hundred lifetimes." They think they are telling the truth, which makes them honest, though I am yet to see a love as long as time. I also hear their darker desires.

"Please, God, why won't it end?" "If only I could close my eyes and never ever wake up."

Consciousness is unceasing, and I don't judge. The young in body aren't as free as the old, even if age is in body only. Maybe if the young were merely landscape, like me, or if they could know what it's like to be a tree. It is possible to live for thousands of years undisturbed by the human condition, or should I say the human affliction? But these young people were never given the chance. They've never had the sardonic gift of an old body. If only...

The Disappearance of Ariel Hassan
Collected by Archival Team Member, Alexander Lopez

Welcome to Room #11 on our tour through the Lost Colony of Desperate. In this room you will find an excerpt of an unfinished memoir manuscript from the novelist Ariel Hassan, as well as artifacts from her life and Desperate investigation. The manuscript was donated to the North Carolina State University special collections library after Hassan's untimely passing. It is currently believed that there was no foul play involved.

Desperate scholars will be interested to know, however, that Hassan's family home was victim to attempted arson prior to her death. The ensuing fire damaged much of her personal records. The section of the manuscript that follows, written after her infamous interview with former Andronika Editor-in-Chief, Calliope Nefter, was left mostly intact, much to the delight of the special collections division.

We are thrilled to present a rare and unvarnished personal account of Hassan's private thoughts and recollections of the days leading up to her interview, as told in her own voice. Scholars of Desperate should be careful to note that our researchers are still working to exhume parts of the journal that remain currently illegible.

Please proceed into the room to view the original documents of Arial Hassan, with accompanying notes from the archivist. After the excerpt from her manuscript you will find an audio icon that, using the audio capability of your glasses, will allow you to listen to the original audio recording of her infamous interview with Calliope Nefter.

FROM THE UNFINISHED MEMOIR OF ARIEL HASSAN

— I remember that the building was cold as I navigated its halls. The streets outside blared with the yawping of New York in springtime. This city that had survived so much, continued to scream on like a reincarnated and newborn soul, caught in a cycle of endless beginning and end.

I felt eyes on me as I followed the signs indicating where I should go. The receptionist had been somewhat cold, barely looked at me, just muttered something about following the queues. I'd always dreamed of being in this building, and then as I stood there, walking toward the room I was about to inhabit, talking to the woman I was about to meet. I remember that I froze a minute, questioning what I'd brought with me, and if I'd perhaps made an awful mistake.

I'd often fantasized about walking in a forced leisure past *these* people. I tried my best to keep my cool. The gatekeepers. How I envied them. The brilliant ones. I was surprised at how few there really were in the end. Just a few dozen, impeccably dressed, busied at desks topped with endless piles of important seeming paper. How few hands held the power that so many sought in the end. That power that I was seeking, too.

I had been surprised when my agent had even called me for this interview. I'd dropped the milk I was holding at Charlie's, the bodega around the corner from my flat, which I rented for the subsidized state price of eight hundred a month in Flushing. I felt a far cry from the skyscrapers of the bustling city, whose heart I now wandered inside.

"Why me?" I'd asked Margaret, my kindly agent, who'd taken such a risk when investing in me.

"Honestly, I don't know," she'd answered, with no attempt to spare my feelings. "But she asked for you specifically."

This word, *specifically*, had haunted the days that led up to my arrival. What could Calliope Nefter possibly want with a young writer like me? I hadn't even published yet in the magazine. My first book wasn't even out until next year at the small house who'd taken me on. It wasn't like I was some rising star. I had no online presence. I was far closer to the unknown man in the alley who watched me with pity as my milk carton exploded at Charlie's, than I was to the halls of a place like that.

It was all so unexplainable and strange.

The guests on *that* radio show were usually titans of their field, at the climax of a long and storied career, and then, somehow, *me*. Little Ariel Hassan. From Flushing. Calliope Nefter had wanted to meet *me*. A strange and ominous thing indeed. The anatomy of a death foretold, perhaps.
I'd half expected the halls to be plated in some sort of golden sheen. I'd always imagined what it would feel like to stand inside those rooms. And in the imaginings there was always something sparkling. A lightness to the bodies. A crispness to the air. The power that it must all hold. Being so close to the beating heart of the written word.

I should note that Andronika magazine had, to anyone who knew anything, been the principal publisher of top artistic talent since 1754, when the magazine was commissioned by the King of England, prior to even the founding of the United States. Its stated purpose was to celebrate the literary titans (and rising stars in the making) on a global scale, who were telling stories that would sculpt and meld and influence public opinion for the betterment of "collective humanity". However, the more I researched the history of Andronika, the more I learned that its true founder had been somewhat ambiguous. The official decree from King George's court had mentioned the name of what everyone assumed to be a Lord, a Christopher Franny. I couldn't find any other historical record of him, apart from his mention in the royal decree.

I'd called up an old professor friend who'd given me access to their universities' special collections library. I'd known they were featuring an exhibit about Desperate and that there were letters that had been collected and newly restored. They were such sad things, sandwiched alongside medical reports and the infamous Herzog photograph. I had to be escorted into the room, wear gloves, the whole thing, but I'd found something then, that name again, Franny.

Do you know sometimes things don't feel coincidental? It's unexplainable, I had no proof, but something in me believed that the Franny from the Colony, that the midwife so desperately applauded, who seems to have just slipped from the historical records of Desperate all-together, it seems that she might be the Franny mentioned in King Henry's decree. But how would that be possible? That would make her hundreds of years old? But if the legends of Desperate were to be believed…. People would probably call me crazy for even saying something. Is that what I was about to do? Go on the air and admit to being a crackpot conspiracy theorist?

[NOTE FROM THE ARCHIVIST: This next section of Ariel's manuscript is quite charred. I've tried my best to decipher, but in the interest of presenting my findings, I will summarize what I believe to be her key points. Hassan goes on for some time about Andronika. "By the time of my birth", she begins , "the magazine was so old and respected, had morphed and updated so logically and kindly with the times, that it, unlike almost any other pillar of the old world, still held esteem with the masses and the elites alike. Being printed amongst its pages didn't just introduce you to the literati, it inducted you into their private and hallowed world. It introduced you en masse to a literary society at large and all at once scooped you up and away from everything that had ever held you back. At least, this is what I had always been led to believe." It appears Hassan was a scholar of Andronika in her collegiate years at CUNY. She smartly noted the Franny comparison, a claim which has yet to be properly verified, but has, since the discovery of this manuscript, yielded intense public speculation. The estate of Calliope Nefter has issued no public statement as to the text of what follows.]

FROM THE MANUSCRIPT OF ARIEL HASSAN
CONT'D

I studied this phenomenon in my collegiate years. The massive forces that determined which books and authors got read over the millennia and which didn't. There had been a mogul in the later half of the 21st century with the last name Godfrey. Many scholars during the time were predicting the end of literacy and credit her along with other public figures of colossal renown in drumming up just enough of the sales and solicitation of fine literature to keep the market afloat during chaotic economic times. Though nothing can hold a candle to the influence of Andronika. Nobody has ever, since its inception, done anything close to what this journal is capable of. It has the ability to start riots in the streets, topple autocracies, radicalize or de-radicalize entire countries. It is the thing universally watched, the one thing that is kept safe from the dismantling hands of the ever changing public desire.

It is important to note that literature can actually never die, but nobody, not even I knew this back then, and so in the tradition of theories that govern all things, I was destined to fret just as my granddaughter and great great-grandchildren would fret, that the world itself is burning up before our eyes, and that it never will be renewed fully.

But all things lost can become found again.

It is also important to note that all young people are like this in perpetuity, and should largely not be listened to about such matters, whenever possible, as nearly all systems, good or bad, find a way forward. Even weeds grow through the toxic soil of what was once the midland prairies of this nation undone. I wish I could have known this inherently then, but I was victim to the predilections of human influence and the ignorance of youth.

Andronika itself is the best proof though, that some things can never truly die. The publication survived the killing seasons. It seemed to emerge again and again from the ashes of a planet unhinged. During the tyrannical autocracies, it proliferated underground, during the climate disasters, it went digital, and now, in this briefly stable liminal space between the old world and whatever might survive in the new, Andronika is still here, beating like the human heart, watching over the world, offering itself like food to the beggar in the street, whose empty belly burns with hunger.

I liked then to imagine that Andronika would forever exist, even long after my death and the death of everyone I have ever loved. That at the corner store in the sky ten thousand years from now, for just four pieces of whatever currency they might someday use, that you too could escape into the unknown worlds of The Andronika Journal, whose stories gave voice to the voiceless and power to those who truly needed it.

When picking the story for my interview, I had quite a hard time. Should I pick something classic? I knew some authors who would pick an unknown story by a ubiquitously famous writer. That was always a very smart choice. But the story that came to me was one that my mother had recommended. My mother, that sweet simple woman, who on the phone had said, "Darling, just pick that story you loved as a girl about tree rings."

Even the mention of it had done something to me. I'd felt a *feeling* like a gust of wind or the moment when wine takes you over and you feel your body soften into itself. The familiarity of ease.

I'd heard the words of this, that hallowed story, first as a little girl. It had been so different from the types of things the magazine usually published. Asynchronous to the brand, if you could have a brand for such a long running and ever changing publication. Yet, even in its simplicity I had recognized the supreme power of the words, as if it were an incantation, a spell cast upon me, a child destined to become a woman, made manifest through the words of not a story, but a prediction, a prophecy, a *confession*.

I'd wondered if maybe it was this story that had made me a writer in the first place. Maybe it was curling up in the lap of a mother who smiled down at me with large white teeth and whispered the legend of the tree's breathing that made me feel the power of its words. I could remember the sensation of the sentences crawling their way through my veins, like caterpillars up a vine. I could remember the feeling deep in the city of my soul, an unknown figure turning the street lamps on in my heart, one by one by one.

The story had *made me* in a way. It had shown me that what I held in my mind was absolutely possible. Because suddenly, I could see it. Everything illuminated.

Naturally, I'd become a bit obsessed with the author. A relatively unknown, yet surprisingly prolific woman, who'd mostly remained quite private.

The author, C.J. Bradley, had become temporarily and most briefly famous in her long running career for a dystopian novel imagining a planet, very similar to ours, where all men and all women were forbidden from bearing children. Instead, within the world of the text, they were grown — harvested really — in a lab. Forced to exist in the world as their most genetically superior selves. The self that was untouchable, formidably immutable. The type of self that knew not the struggles of normal life, but instead the tacit doldrum tones of a life scientifically perfected.

The novel had been a sensation and the writer had, to my delight, been surprisingly coy about her newfound fame. Unaccustomed or unconvinced about its meaning. She often would refuse public interviews or press of any kind. She'd say, often through an agent, who nobody to my knowledge could ever locate in person, that she instead preferred to remain anonymous and keep the lives of her family and herself a totally private affair.

Online there had been speculation. Rumors. Outrageous things. That perhaps she was one of the surviving members of a long destroyed colony called Desperate. The rumor was ridiculous. Debunked. Ridiculed even. Nobody had survived that catastrophe. At least that's what I'd always been told. The idea was simply outrageous. Suspiciously so. That someone could've survived such an extinction? It just wasn't possible.

But then, this story of the tree.

This singular story, whispered almost in confession, that perhaps C.J. Bradley *had* gone by other names, *had* lived other lives, like the rings of the tree that she traces, the tree that like Bradley too was sentient, sturdy and steadfast in a way that nobody else on earth had ever been. And I had to wonder, had C.J. existed for far more years than she was letting on? Had she ever gone by other names?

It wasn't entirely original. It has circulated in the chatrooms and in some academic circles for ages. However, despite this, it wasn't something taken seriously in high literary circles. And still, knowing this, it was C.J. Bradley's story that I chose to talk about on the Andronika Radio Hour with Calliope Nefter, indisputably the most terrifying and powerful titan of literary acclaim alive in the world today. I knew she might eat me alive.

Calliope had been Editor-in-Chief of Andronika for longer than I had even been alive. Seeing her, in human form, just a mere woman was almost unbearable. She was so small, frail even, just sitting there, smiling up at me, motioning for me to sit down.

It felt like some elaborate, sedated, strangely forbidden charade. As if I was seeing the future of a destiny I had not yet earned. Sleeping in the bed of a house I could never afford. And as I walked into the room without pause and sat down upon the throne of my new life, I thought perhaps that I might be smiling for the very last time.

[NOTE FROM THE ARCHIVIST: What follows is the excerpted transcript of Ariel Hassan's interview with Calliope Nefter]

ANDRONIKA MAGAZINE'S RADIO HOUR

CALLIOPE: Live from the Andronika Magazine Radio Hour, I'm your host, Calliope Nefter.

[NOTE FROM THE ARCHIVIST: A tape rings out here of pre-recorded people shouting out with glee, cheering and clapping.]

CALLIOPE: Each month, we invite a writer to choose a story from our archives to discuss. This month we are going to read "Tree Rings", selected for you by Ariel Hassan.

Ariel, how are you today?

ARIEL: Hello Ms. Nefter, it's such an honor to be here. You have no idea.

CALLIOPE: Please, call me Calliope.

CALLIOPE: Go ahead and tell us a bit about the piece you chose for today.

ARIEL: Well, "Tree Rings" is a

story that came out about twenty years ago in the magazine and it wasn't terribly popular at the time, but it marked an interesting turn for the representation of science fiction in the magazine, which had been fighting for equal airtime for quite a while, so to speak.

CALLIOPE: Yes, I remember it vividly. Bradley is actually a dear friend of mine. Brilliant woman.

ARIEL: Oh... I'm sorry, I um, I didn't realize.

ARIEL: I was fascinated by it as a girl, I didn't realize you knew her well, sorry... I mean to say... it spoke to me. I didn't mean to say it was...

CALLIOPE: Go on Ariel, you're doing great.

ARIEL: Um, right. I'm sorry. Let me just gather my thoughts. I think it perhaps, the story, maybe represented a hidden truth about the world?

CALLIOPE: How so?

ARIEL: That perhaps there is more than meets the eye? The woman in the story. She seems to have a connection with the tree somehow, as if...maybe I'm reaching a bit here...

but maybe she is the tree? Forever alive, never growing old.

CALLIOPE: That's....an interesting take on it. I'm not sure most people would read it that way. But then again it is somewhat of a fable.

ARIEL: I'm not sure I think it is a fable. I think it is an autobiography. I think it isn't fiction at all.

CALLIOPE: Let's not be silly. You aren't one of those Bradley "truthers" are you? Someone call the History Channel!

ARIEL: *Nervously laughing* Well no, I realize it's a bit out there, but there is rumor and speculation that the tree, that when it's chopped down at the end, and the woman, that faceless woman, who laments life so often and so audibly, that perhaps she is a part of the tree in some integral way. That she is surviving this gutting. That the world is dying around her and she is stuck forever, paralyzed by living, forever awake.

CALLIOPE: That's an interesting take on things.

ARIEL: Well, the tree bears fruit, no? And when she absconds in the end, she bites from an apple that the tree has made and swallows it hard.

Ariel pauses

ARIEL: I think, if I may be so bold, that she's kept the seeds, one of the seeds of immortality that the tree has provided and that she plans to live forever, that anyone with the seeds of the tree can live forever. I think it's a metaphor.

CALLIOPE: Well, that is a very original interpretation, Ariel. I can almost hear the blogosphere and scholarly community of Desperate ravenous with excitement.

ARIEL: But if it is true that she's survived the explosion, why keep it hidden? Why hasn't she given us any answers publicly? I think the people deserve some answers. I think C.J. Barney owes us a public explanation.

[NOTE FROM THE ARCHIVIST: The audio, as the astute scholar of Desperate will note, is dimmed beyond comprehension here, but cutting edge software has allowed us to illuminate imprints of the tonal exchange that follows. It's believed that the final exchange is Calliope Nefter saying, "Do you want to meet her and ask her yourself?"]

***ADDENDUM: Following the interview, which went viral on multiple platforms, the #CJMustSpeak was trending around the world. After decades of silence, the author agreed to accept an invitation to speak publicly about the matter.

The Immortal Interview
Collected by Archival Team Member, Cadwell Turnbull

Dear Exhibition Guest,

Welcome to Room #12 on our tour through the Lost Colony of Desperate. You are nearly at the end of your time with us. We hope you have enjoyed learning more about the lost world of Desperate, NC. Be sure to thank your guides on your way out.

By now you've no doubt seen the infamous interview that captured worldwide attention, but in Room #11 of your interactive tour, relive the suspense and the terror of CJ Bradley's live TV moment, including-never before seen, behind the stage footage. First hand interviews from crew members, and a brand new video interview with Collin Tram's son, James Tram.

Most importantly though, you hold in your hands the official transcript, excerpted from Collin Tram's international best selling book of essays, generously made available by CBS Universal and the estate of Collin Tram, which details the moment of that fateful interview.

You may now proceed into the final room.

"Folks, my next guest is a best-selling and award-winning author of novels and short story collections. Her latest novel, Cherry Wine, is out now. Please welcome, C.J. Bradley!"

Stephen Colbert was slower now as he pushed out from his desk and made the trek to Bradley. Even at age 76, he insisted on getting up to greet the people coming onto his show. Bradley waited at the stage entrance for Colbert where they hugged and exchanged brief words, muted by the jazzy intro music and the cheering audience, before they both took the slow walk back to the desk and couch.

Colbert's background hadn't changed in thirty years. It was that same panorama of New York City at night, the sky a ghostly blue from all those skyscraper lights. He still used traditional cameras—no camera drones buzzing overhead. Everything was comfortably familiar, a time capsule for his viewing audience, who'd grown into old age with him.

As they sat, Colbert leapt into questions. "So, tell me, is your first name Cherry?"

C.J. Bradley chuckled. "No, it's Charlotte, but I see you've been talking to some of my fans."

"No one needs to talk to them," Colbert said. "They're loud enough on their own."

The audience laughed.

When Colbert was younger, his voice would sometimes slink down a register and you could hear the rattle at the edges of his words. Now it was all rattle, bruised vocal cords that had hardened around the hurt. He was hunching in his chair, the now characteristic bend to his back visible in his nice suit. It was the full beard that made it all work. Like Letterman before him, he'd gone white, and it made him look both distinguished and trustworthy.

"Well, this must be an elaborate troll, then," Colbert said. "You've now written a whole book about Desperate."

"It's no secret that Tree Rings was inspired by Desperate."

"But still, why return to it?"

"Because I'm old," Bradley said. "Impending death has a way of inciting old fascinations." You had to look at Bradley's mouth to tell her true feelings. She had thin eyebrows that arched steeply as if in constant surprise. But her lips were curled in a clever smirk. "Maybe I'm trolling a little," she admitted.

"But you're focused on Cherry in this one?"

"Yes, the radical child immortal that helped destroy the whole town. It is a story worth telling."

"Are you from Desperate?"

Bradley, for her part, didn't miss a beat. "Of course not."

Sensing an opportunity for a little fun, Colbert took an alternative tact. "Okay," he said, "let's say for the sake of discussion that you were one of the original members of Desperate. How would you explain your birth records and all the evidence that points to you being a mere mortal like the rest of us?"

It was obvious why Bradley accepted the bait. She'd just been invited to speculate about her own existence, to pretend to lie while telling the truth. If she were a member of Desperate how could she resist?

She didn't answer right away. She was too careful for that. "Are you serious?" she asked.

"Dead serious," Colbert said. It was what a studio audience should laugh at, so they did.

"Let's say I am from Desperate," Bradley said. "Why would I have a birth certificate from the 1960s? Well, we did leave the settlement from time to time. The trick was to lay the seeds for future expeditions decades ahead, sometimes centuries.

Build future histories for yourself and other Desperates. Birth certificates are easy if you plan ahead. I have at least four birth certificates. I have death certificates, too. Sometimes I was my own mother. We could be anyone we wanted."

"Like Christopher Franny," Colbert asked.

Bradley smiled. "Sure."

"That's a really good story," Colbert said. "Convenient, but really good." He tapped the desk signaling the end of the hypothetical adventure. "So, what do you do in your free time when you're not defending your mortality?"

"Wait," she said. "Just wait a minute."

Some of the sharp eyes in the audience might've noticed how Bradley's mouth twisted into something pained. The clever smirk had disappeared.

"Aren't you going to ask me what is at the center of me?" she asked him. Colbert stared at Bradley, and it was clear that he didn't remember that in 2018 he'd asked this very question to the then living Malcolm Gladwell. "What is the center of your belief?" he had asked. "What is the core of Malcolm Gladwell? If I cut you open and counted the rings, what's that center ring?"

Who knows when Bradley saw the Gladwell interview, but it was the sort of poetic symmetry that would be irresistible to Bradley the writer, some cosmic pattern showing itself.

To Colbert the question was completely out of the blue, so he stumbled out a response: "If you want me to, I will."

Bradley did not explain herself. "Why don't you see for yourself," she said. "Cut me open."

Again, he didn't understand what she was getting at. "What?"

"You know about Revision, don't you? We can put this all to rest. Cut me open. Count the rings."

Colbert laughed. It was desert dry and his face betrayed him. "No, no," he said. He sat in the moment, her eyes on him, those eyes filled with need. She had the brightest blue eyes, and long black eyelashes.

Bradley ruffled in her purse and pulled out the pocket knife. The show lights reflected off the smooth polymer. She flicked it open, snapped the sharp blade into position, and rested the open knife on the desk between them.

"Oh, God," Colbert said.

If it was another host, the interview would've ended there. Maybe even an earlier Colbert would've stopped everything. But this Colbert had lost so much, had outlived so many of the people he loved. He'd also outlasted his contemporaries.

No Kimmel. No Fallon. Just Colbert, still working, trying to chase away death.

A moment like this didn't come along often, if ever.

Throughout all this, Bradley had this wild-eyed look about her. She could've done the deed herself if she wanted to, cut open her own wrists or neck. But I suspect she wanted someone to share in it with her. She'd planted her roots in this old man with his bent back and quiet sadness.

"Do it," she dared him.

"I won't," Colbert said. And then with more strength: "I won't do that. But I'll listen. Whatever you want to say." He reached out and slowly pulled the knife to him. Bradley did not protest.

"There's no one left," she said. "No one in the whole world."

And then she cried. It was too raw and discomforting to be good television. But Colbert held her hand and sat with her the whole time.

After a while, she collected herself. The conversation turned to outlasting loved ones. "When you're very old," Bradley said, "most of the people you know are dead." Somewhere within those final minutes they both started to treat the entire melodrama as if it was just the normal distress of old age. Neither of them acknowledged what it really was: a confession.

The Colbert interview came with renewed speculation, but I like to think about what Bradley did directly after the interview, when she was all alone and didn't need to pretend for anyone.

I picture her at her front door, ruffling in her bag for her keys—she still uses keys, of course—her hand gently grazing the pocket knife that Colbert returned to her. I can imagine the quiet smile she gives herself as she considers the interview. What a moment that would have been. The whole world watching.

She enters the house slowly. Her knees aren't what they used to be, but how long had she had strong knees, anyway? A blink of the eye, really. No one thinks of what it's like to be old forever. A life perpetually past its prime.

She makes herself dinner. She sits in front of the TV, one of those fold out tables in front of her. She forks little bites of meatloaf into her mouth. She has to be careful with her false teeth. They wear out even if she does not.

It will be awhile before she watches the footage. For now, she has better things to do with her time.

She goes to the little closet in her bedroom, finds the shoe box crammed in the corner under so

many others. The trick is to guard the most precious things with carelessness. She bends over, picks up the worn box.

It does a number on her back, but it has always done that. She considers the pain punishment.

She takes the box over to her bed and sits down to open it. In the box are the things that you might expect. Old documents and photos, most charred beyond recognition. But Bradley remembers everything.

She spends the most time on one photo in particular. She has to be gentle so it doesn't break apart in her hand. It was an early Kodachrome, from when Oliver worked at Kodak helping to revolutionize color film. They had to mail it to Kodak to get developed. On the edge of the photo she can still see the vibrant red of Agathe's hair in the midday sun. Everything else she has to fill in with her mind. Isaiah's toothy grin. Oliver's lanky frame and mess of hair. And Gertie Lane in her fresh pigtails, a defiant glare at the camera.

She was on one of her long afternoon walks when it happened. She felt the ground shake and watched the smoke curl up into the waiting sky. She'd known they were planning something, had watched them with curiosity, even amusement. And then she'd brought the matter to Barry at the school. She should've done more.

None of them were her true children. Her son died on the ship coming into this new world. Her daughter died across the ocean somewhere in that slippery time of the early settlement. Still, she considered the whole town her children, the ageless ones and the aged, the still photographs and the moving pictures. All dust now.

Her punishment is living. She is waiting for the sun to eat the earth. To cut her open. Count the rings.

The Manifest
Collected by Archival Team Members
Jendayi Brooks-Flemister & Kayla Rutledge

Welcome to Room #13 on our tour through the Lost Colony of Desperate.
This last and final section of your Field Guide to Desperate is of particular
delight to the archival department. Never before has an official manifest
been released to the public containing known names of Desperate residents,
but due to recent de-classifications with the U.S. Government and ongoing
increase in public interest, finally, you have in your hands the known citizens
of Desperate.

We hope you have enjoyed your time with us. Please consider purchas-
ing something from the giftshop on your way out. All proceeds help the
museum staff to continue bringing you exciting work such as what you've
experienced today. Pay special attention to our Desperate stickers, they've
been a real hit with our guests!

With much gratitude,

The Archival Division,
The Lost Colony of Desperate: The Interactive Exhibition

KNOWN CITIZEN MANIFEST OF DESPERATE, NORTH CAROLINA

Alami, Agatha
Alami, Osman
Ansoma, Anselm
Ansoma, Unknown
    (mother to P)
Ansoma, Petra
Branscomb, Unknown
    (father to C & D)
Branscomb, Unknown
    (mother to C & D)
Branscomb, Charlie
Branscomb, Davey
Cooper, Unknown
    ("Foreseer")
Everstone, Lily
Gillyweed, Anna
Gillyweed, Barry
Gillyweed, Unknown
    (mother)
Gillyweed, Norman
Gillyweed, Ondine
Gillyweed, Petunia
Gillyweed, Quincy

Gold, Esther
Gold, Levi
Gold, Estye
Gold, Ivan
Jakes, Unknown
    ("Foreseer")
Lane, Unknown
    (father to E & G)
Lane, Unknown
    (mother to E & G)
Lane, Essi
Lane, Gertie
Lawson, Unknown
    ("Preacher")
Ledbetter, Franny
Macabre, Oliver
Ming, Unknown
Patters, Unknown
Patters, Unknown
Patters, Isaiah
Pryce, Unknown
    ("Foreseer")
Rumstead, Lillian

Rumstead, Unknown
    (husband)
Sambutina, John
Sambutima, Unknown
    (mother to N & P)
Sambutina, Naomi
Sambutina, Peter
Sena, Tati
Trout, Geoffrey
Trout, Ginny
Trout, Samuel
Trout, Wilhelmina
Valencia, Unknown
    (father to O & V)
Valencia, Unknown
    (mother to O & V)
Valencia, Olivia
Valencia, Viola
Unknown, August

We hope you have enjoyed spending your day with us here at the special collections division as we navigated the Lost Colony of Desperate. We are deeply grateful for your patronage. And remember, what is lost may become found once more, through grit, determination and the collective effort of focused minds, who are dedicated to telling the truth above all else.

With gratitude,

The Archival Staff at the Lost Colony of Desperate: The Interactive Exhibition
Cadwell Turnbull
Jendayi Brooks-Flemister
Isaac Green
Misha Lazzara
Jesse Wang
Catey Christiansen
Michael Ivory
Elyse Rudemiller
Kayla Rutledge
Ali Saleh
Alexander Lopez
Franny ;-)
Paul Watts-Offret

THIS CONCLUDES THE FIELD GUIDE
TO THE INTERACTIVE EXHIBITION

www.ingramcontent.com/pod-product-compliance
Lightning Source LLC
Chambersburg PA
CBHW030339020726
47493CB00004B/1331